This Coloring Book Belongs To:

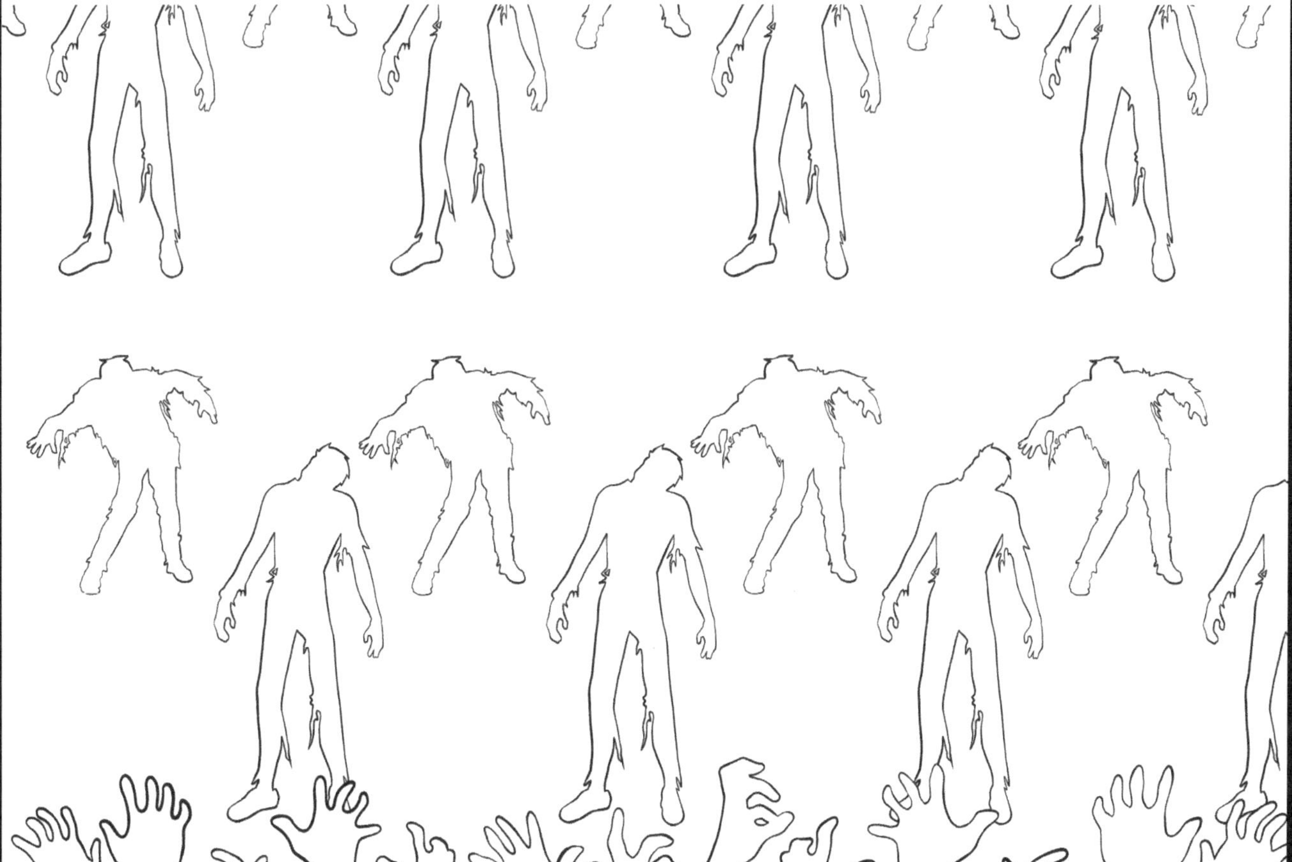

Written and Illustrated by J. Miles Moore
www.JoeyMojojo.com Insta: ArtByJMiles

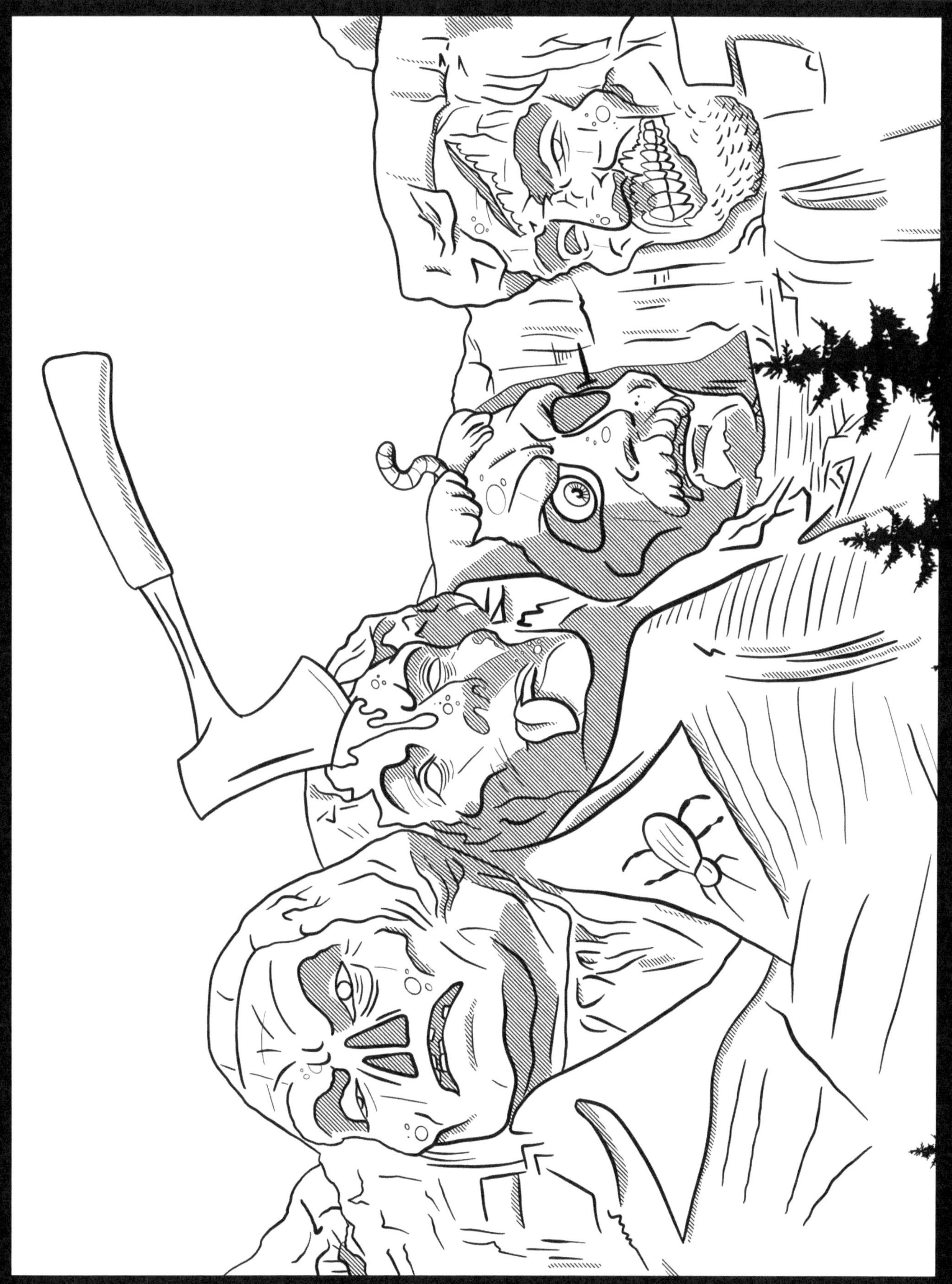

Freedom From The Grave
- Norman RIPwell, 1942

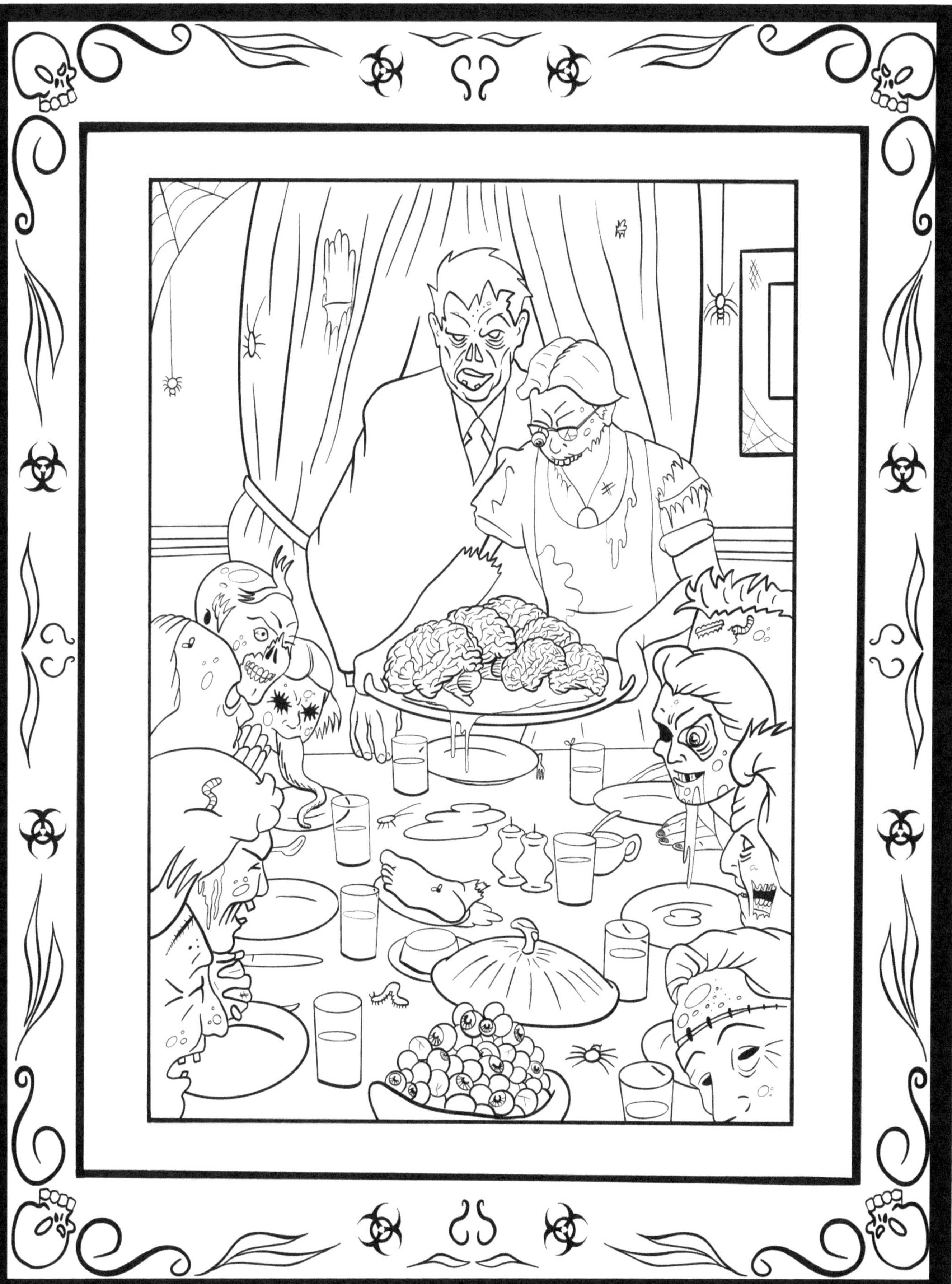

DOODLE: Your rooftop hideout is safe, but very boring. Play ringtoss with old hats on these zombies. Draw as many hats as you can stack on their heads.

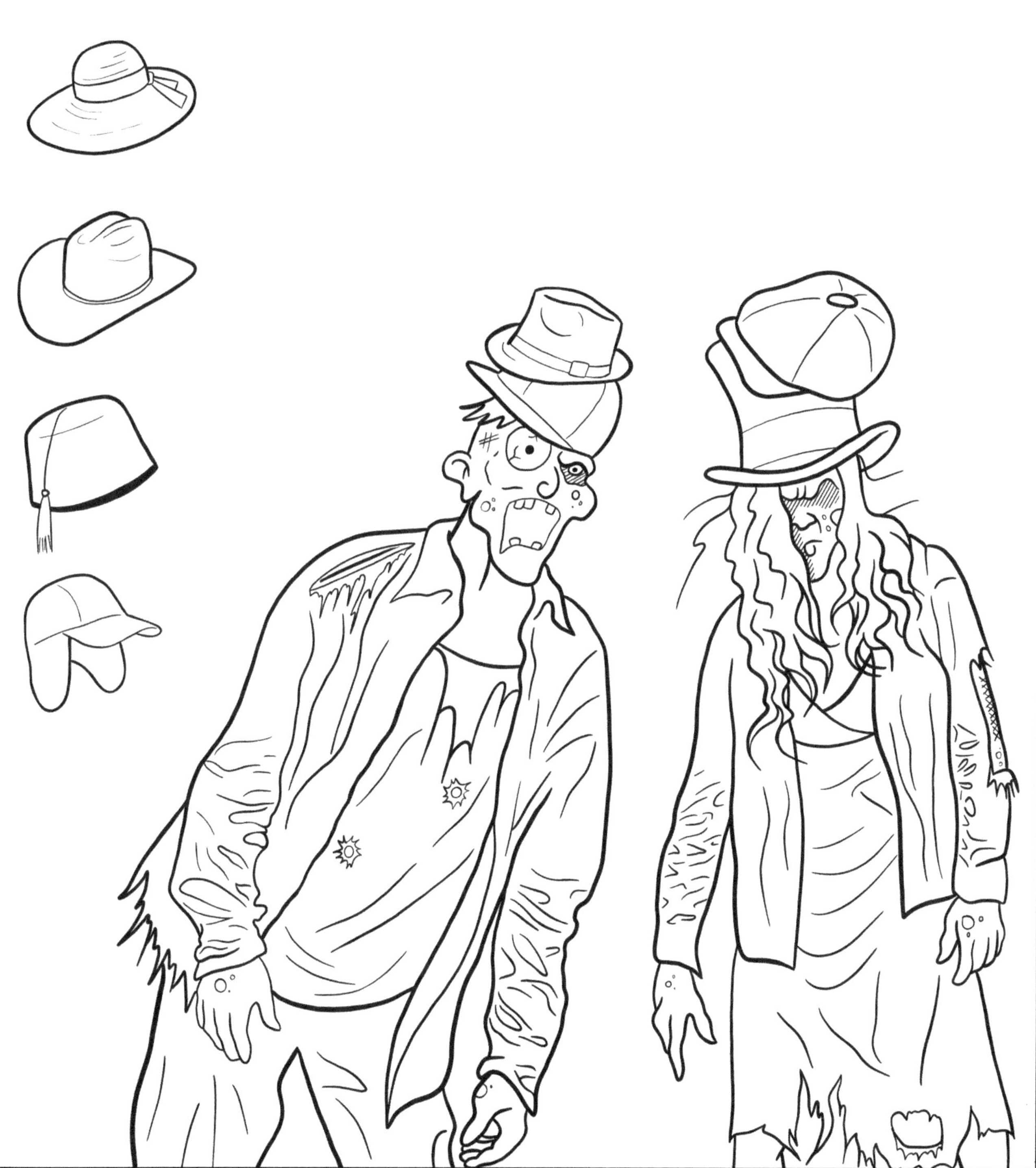

Zombie Road, 1969

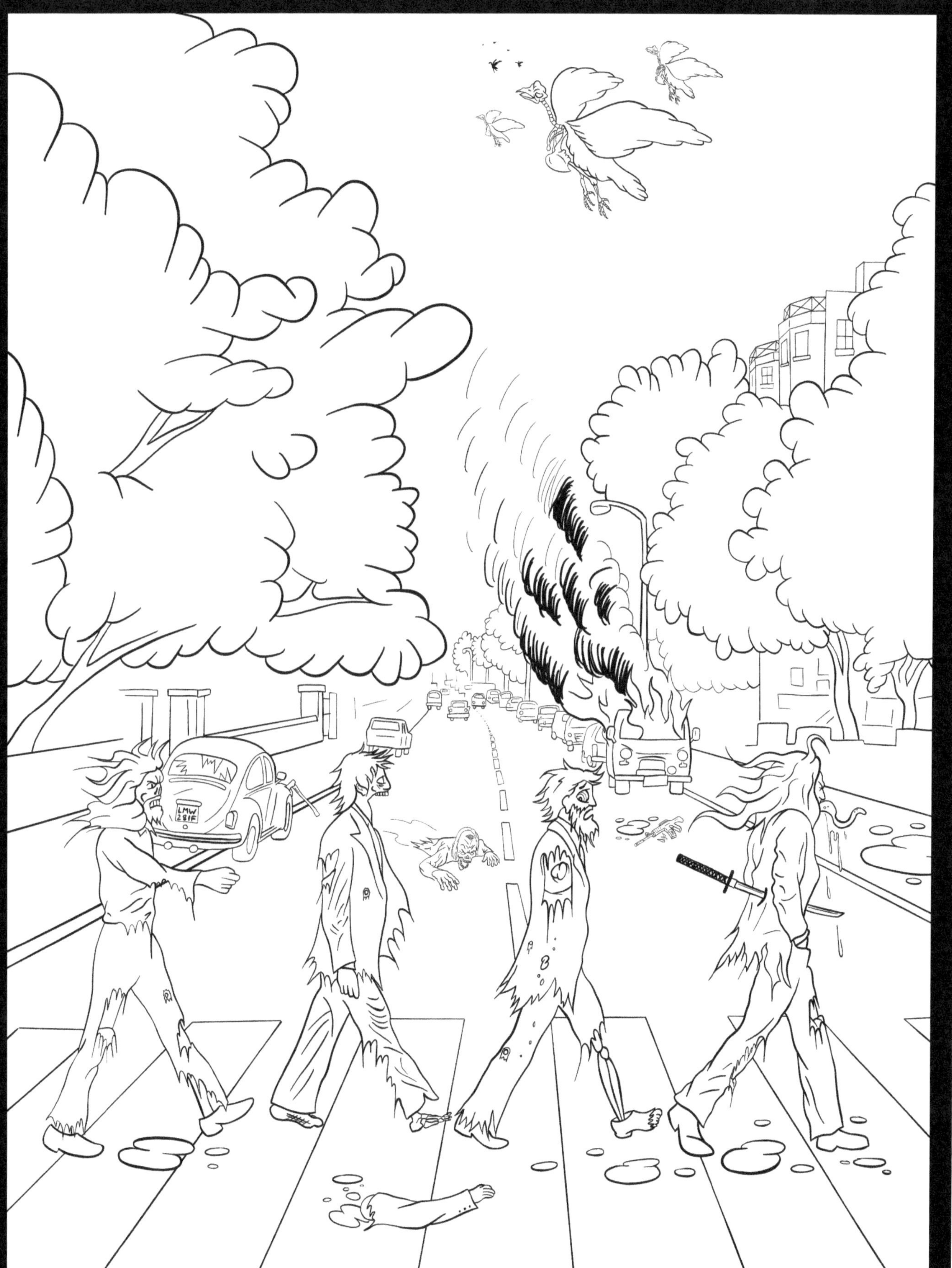

DOODLE: Santa is too busy with his... list. Help him out by decorating his tree with more... ornaments?

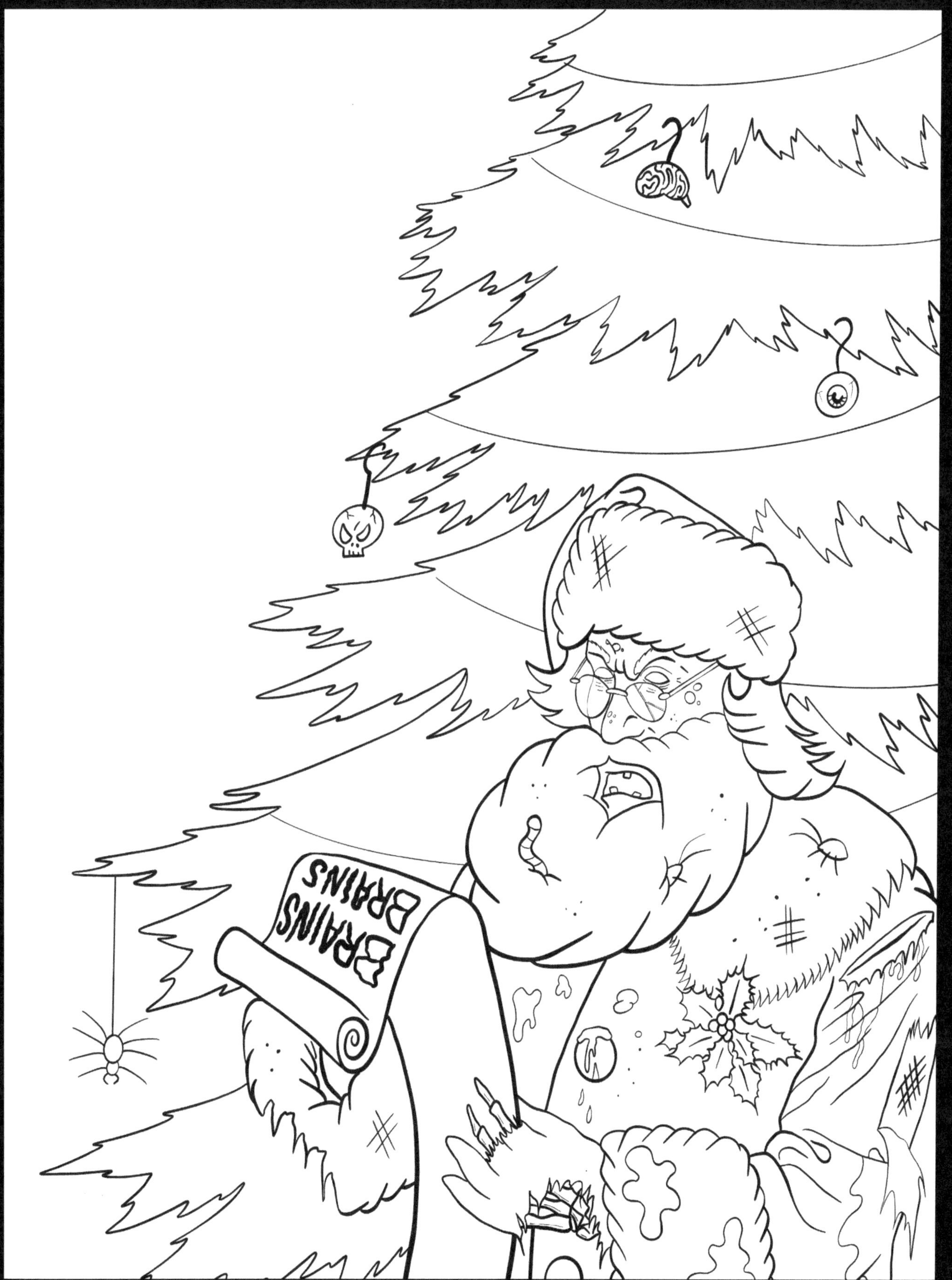
BRAINS
BRAINS

They're tragically delicious!

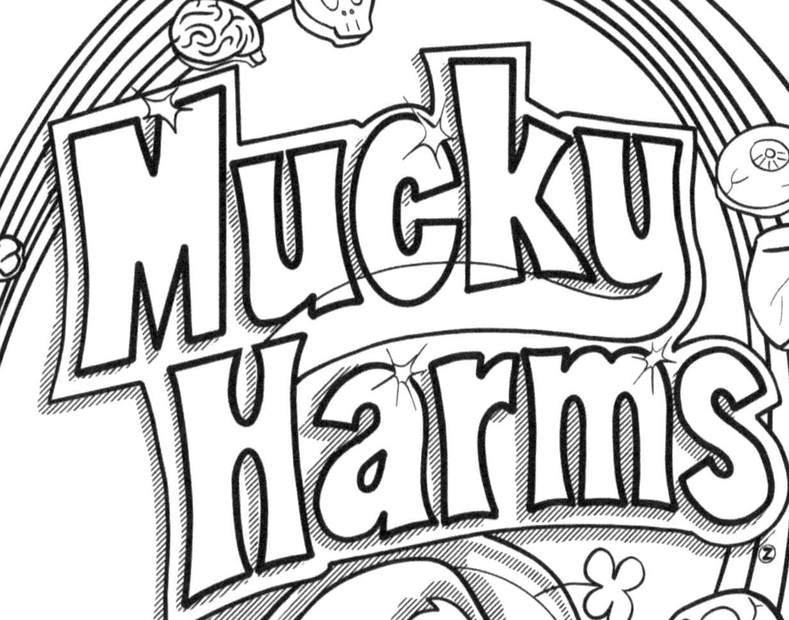
General Chills
Mucky Harms
General Chills
Mucky
Harms
FROSTED BRAINS
AND BRAWS WITH
BRAINMALLOWS
NET WT 666 OZ (13g)

Homage to Return of the Living Dead 2
1988

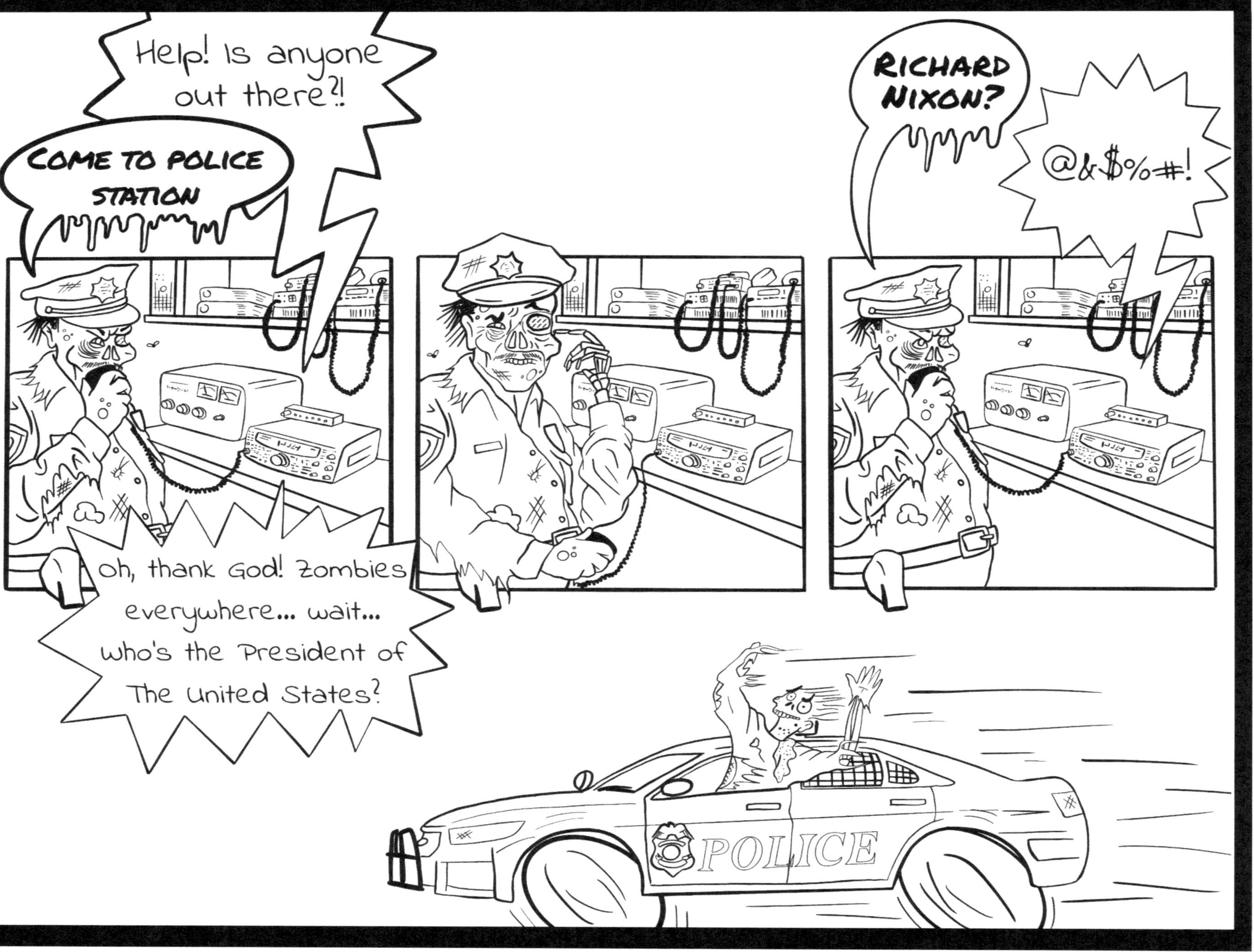
COME TO POLICE STATION
Help! Is anyone out there?!
Oh, thank God! Zombies everywhere... wait... who's the President of The United States?
RICHARD NIXON?
@&$%#!
POLICE

Can you tell me how to get -
how to get to...

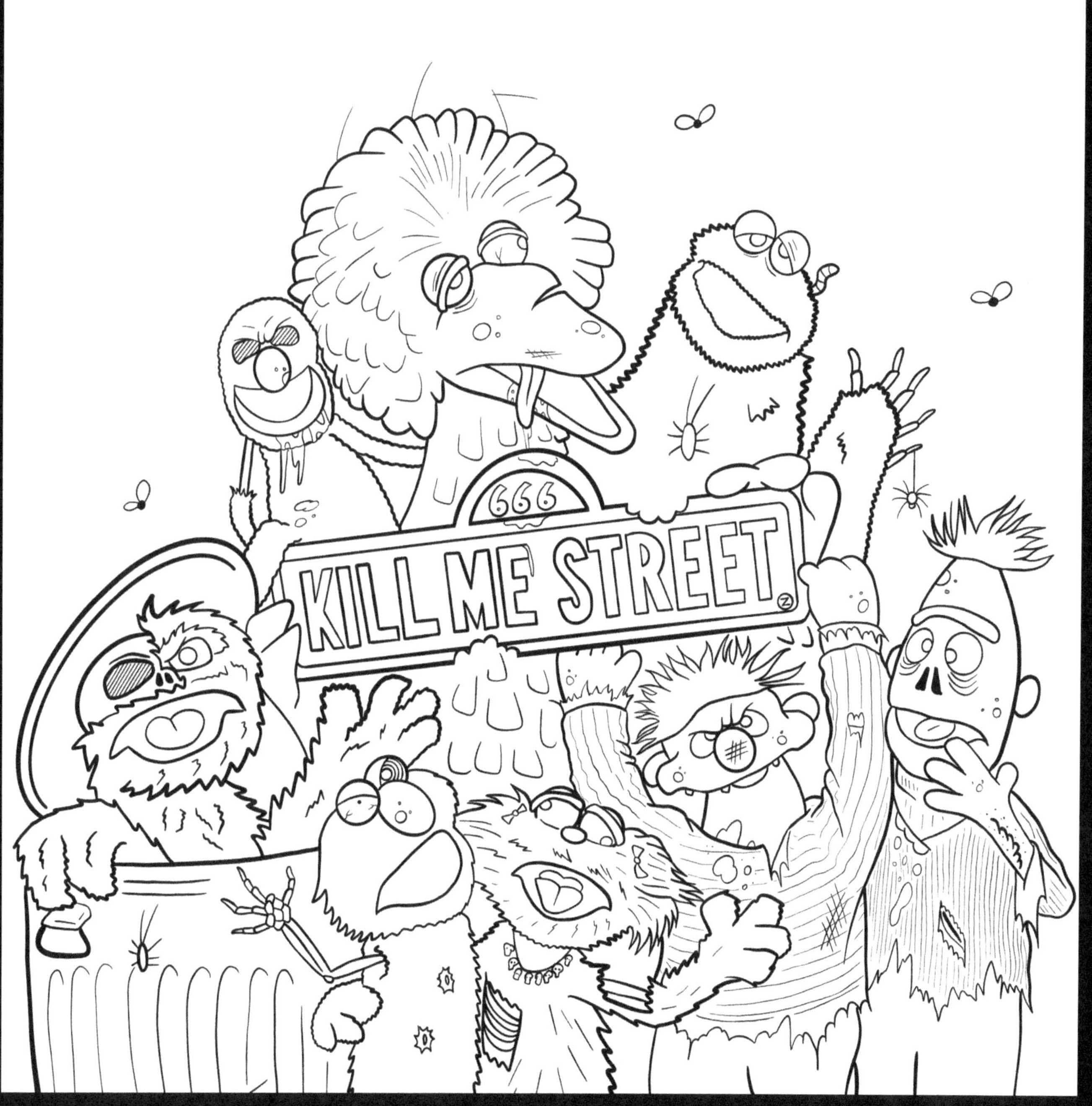
666
KILL ME STREET

We're off to see the wizard,
the wonderful wizard of
AAAAAAAHHHHHZZZZ!!!!!!!

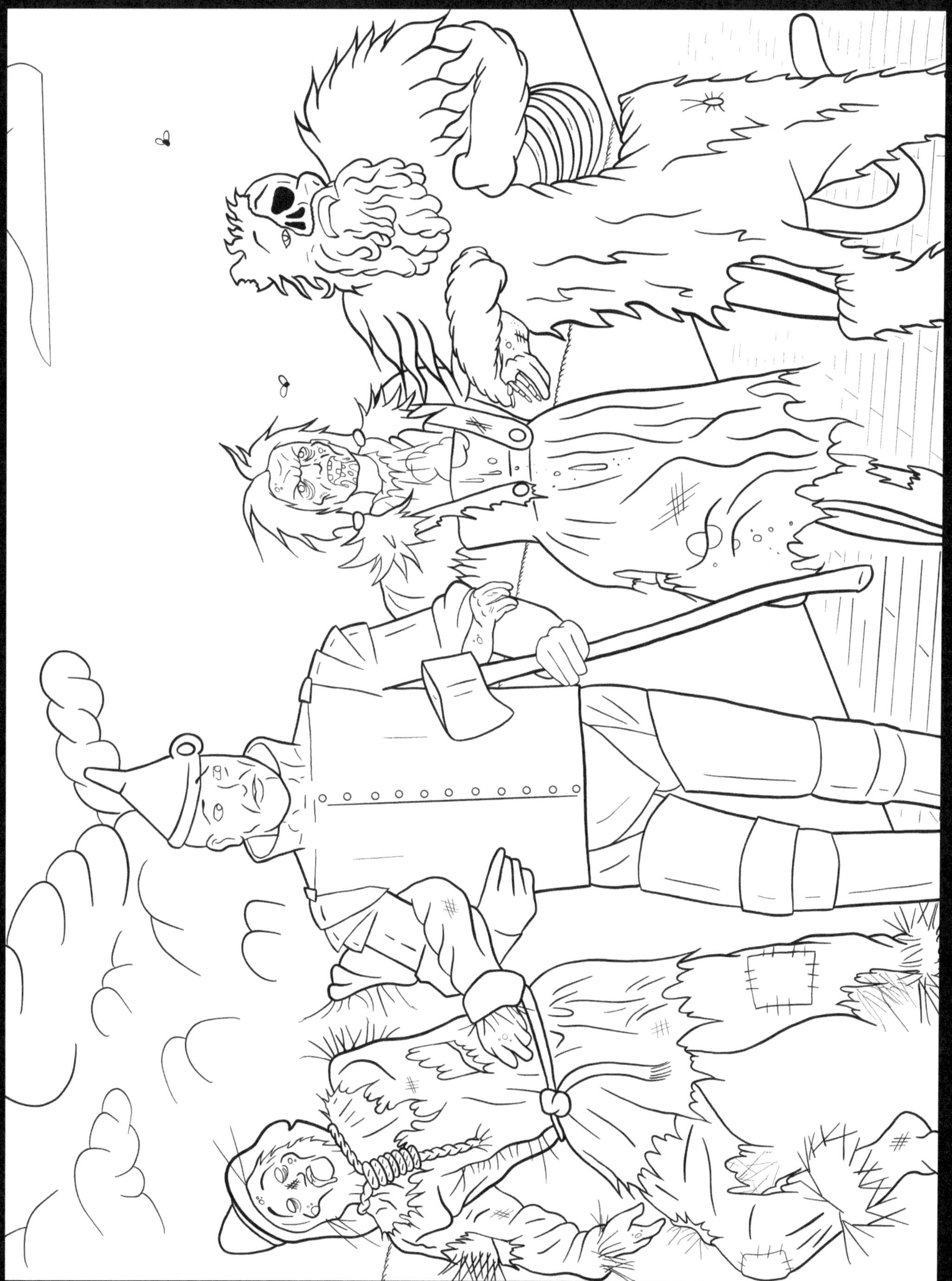

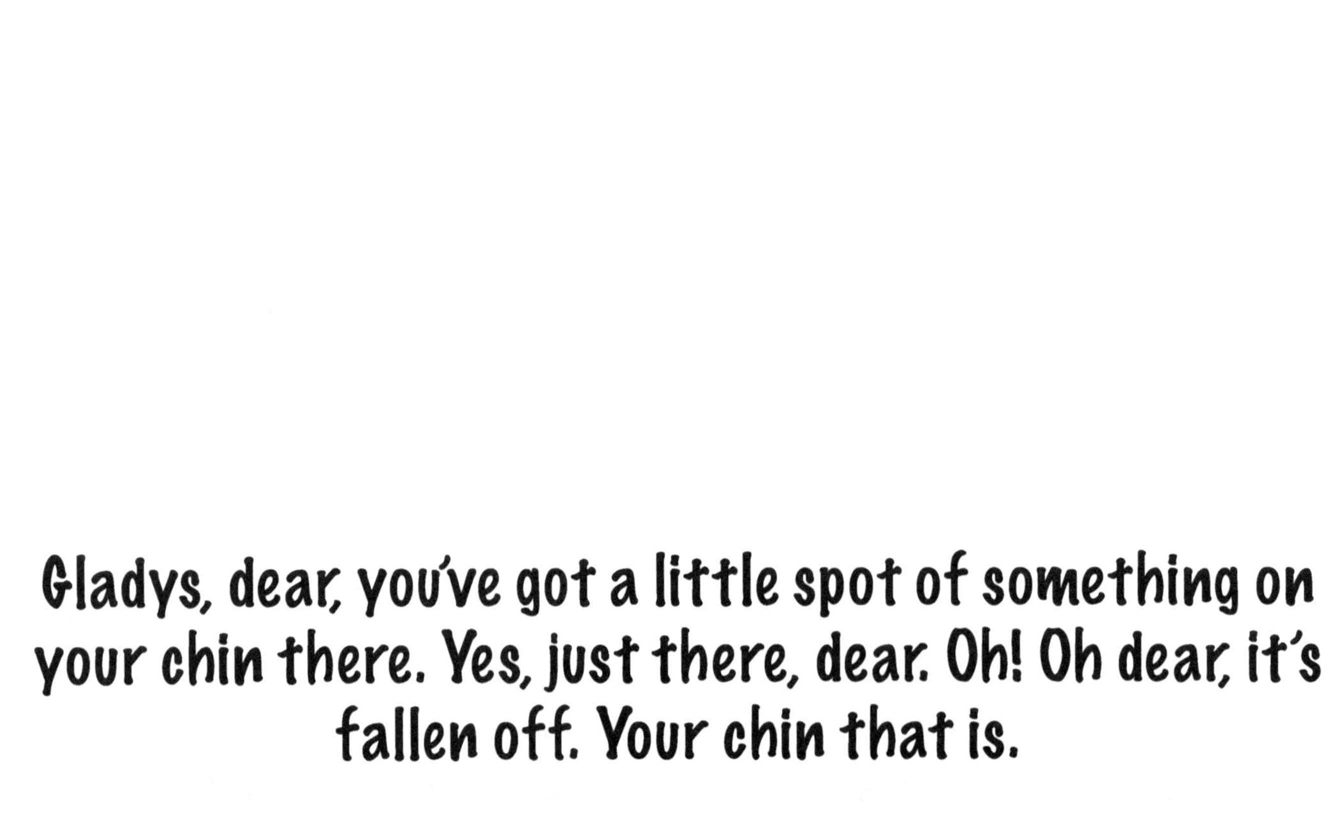

Gladys, dear, you've got a little spot of something on your chin there. Yes, just there, dear. Oh! Oh dear, it's fallen off. Your chin that is.

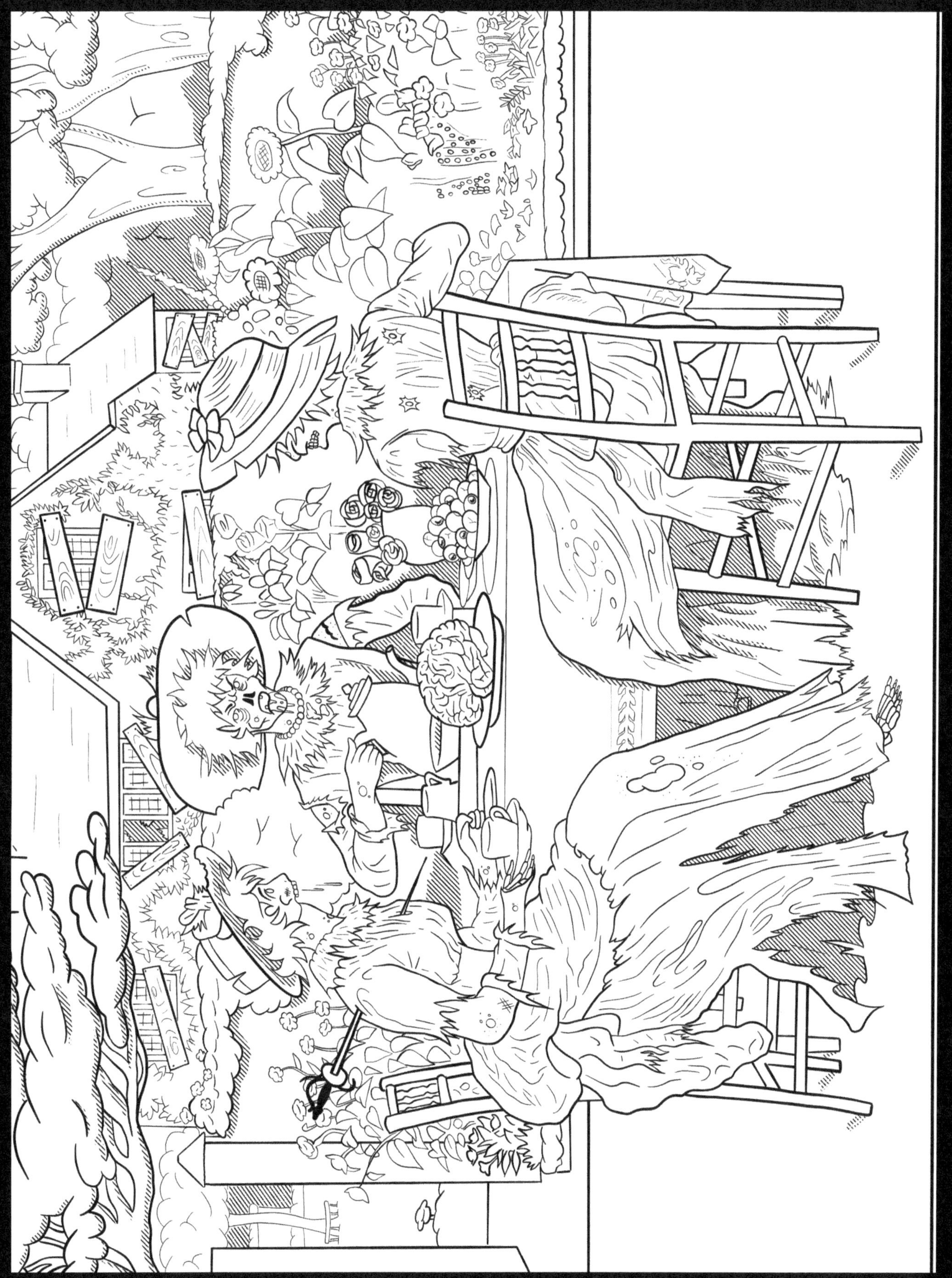

A Taste of Their Own Medicine.

AKA

American Gothic, 1930

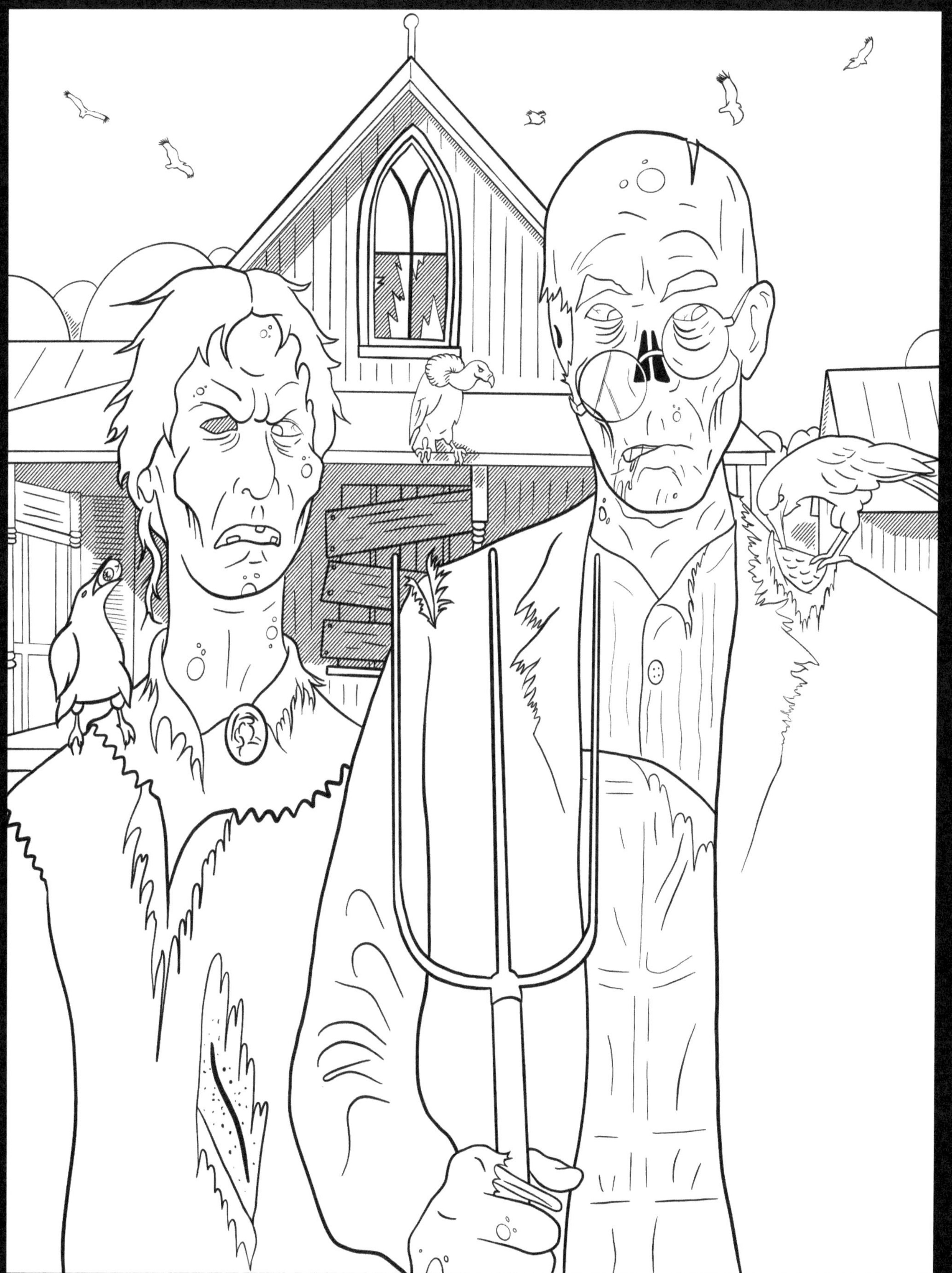

Happy Little Zombies.

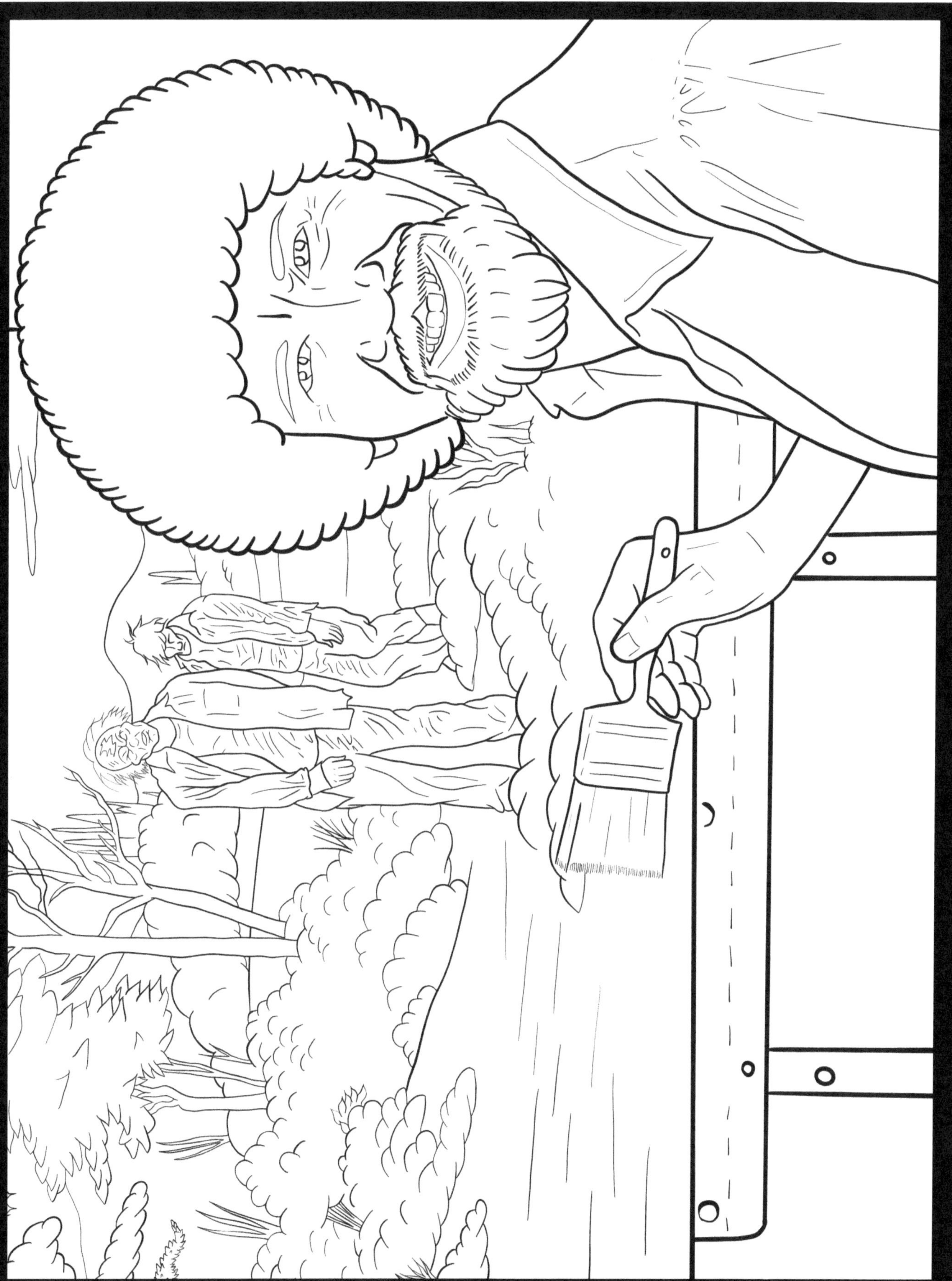

Ah ah ah ah
I'm not alive, I'm not alive
ah ah ah ah AAAAAAAAAAHHHHH!!!!!

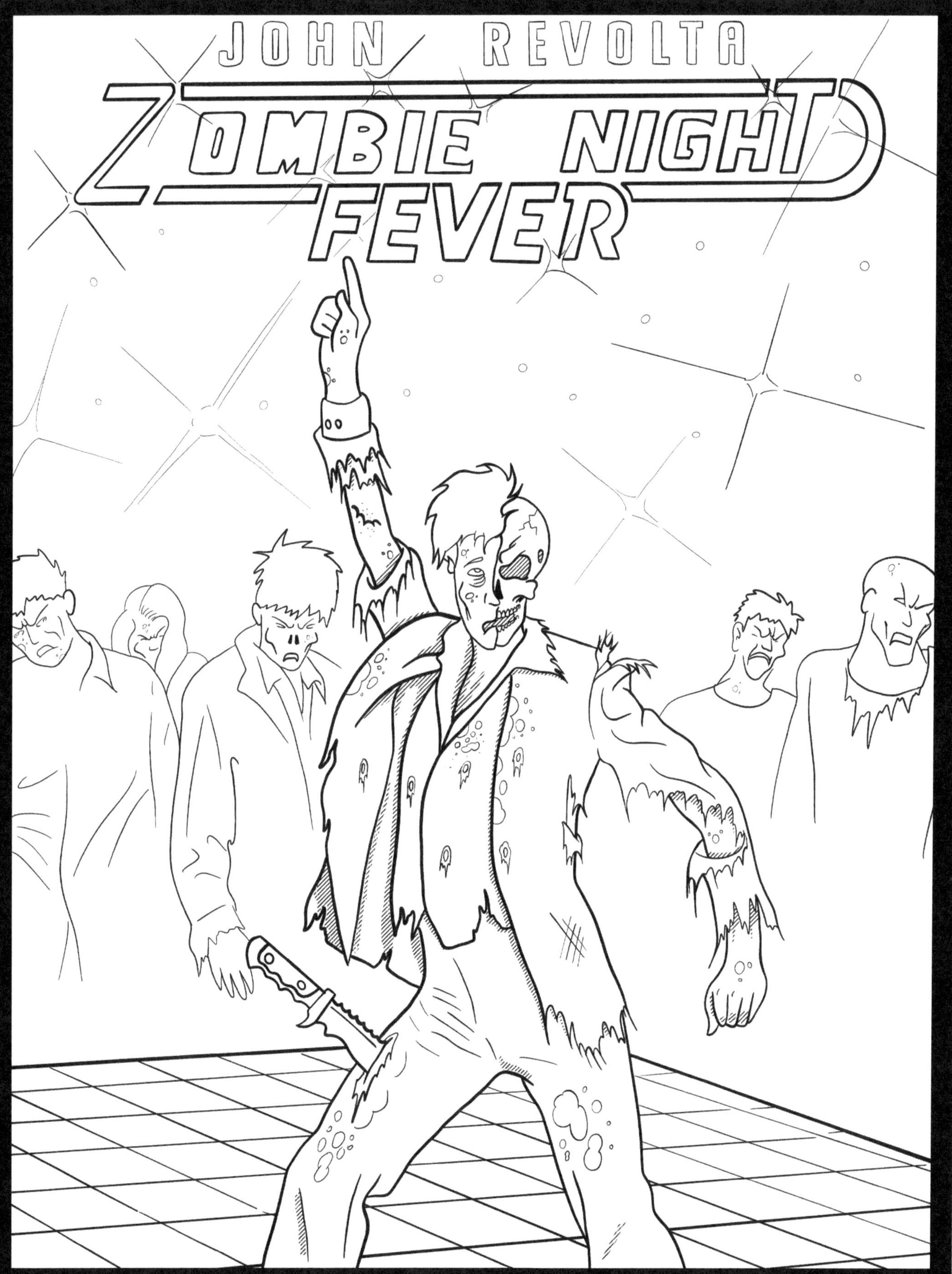
JOHN REVOLTA
ZOMBIE NIGHT FEVER

Fast food? Wasn't fast enough.

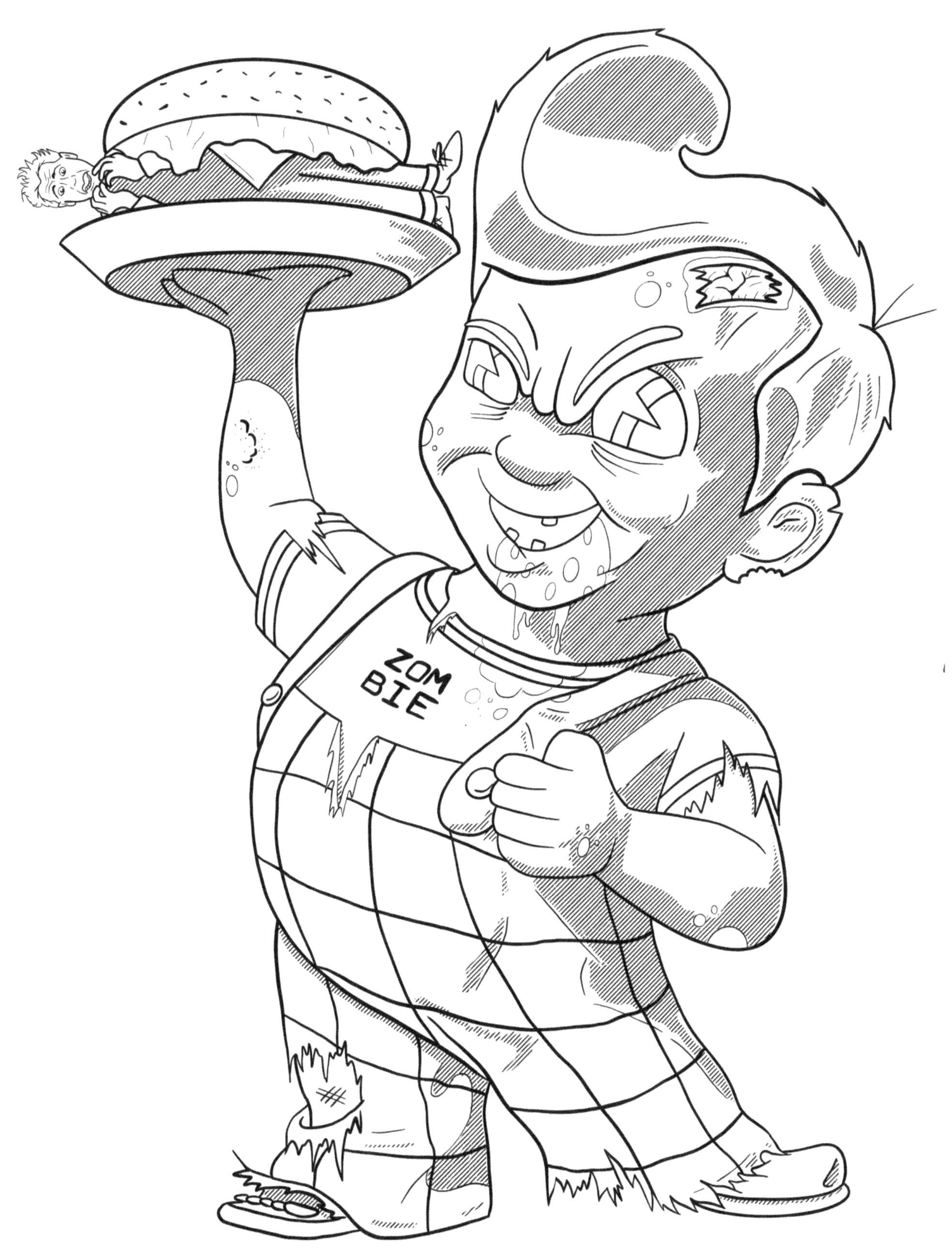
ZOM
BIE

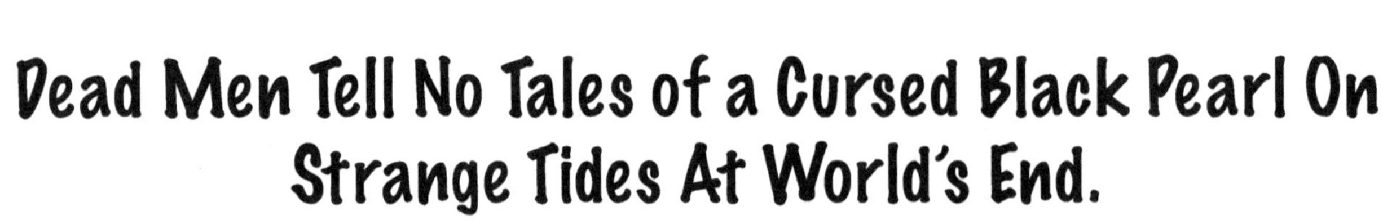
Dead Men Tell No Tales of a Cursed Black Pearl On
Strange Tides At World's End.

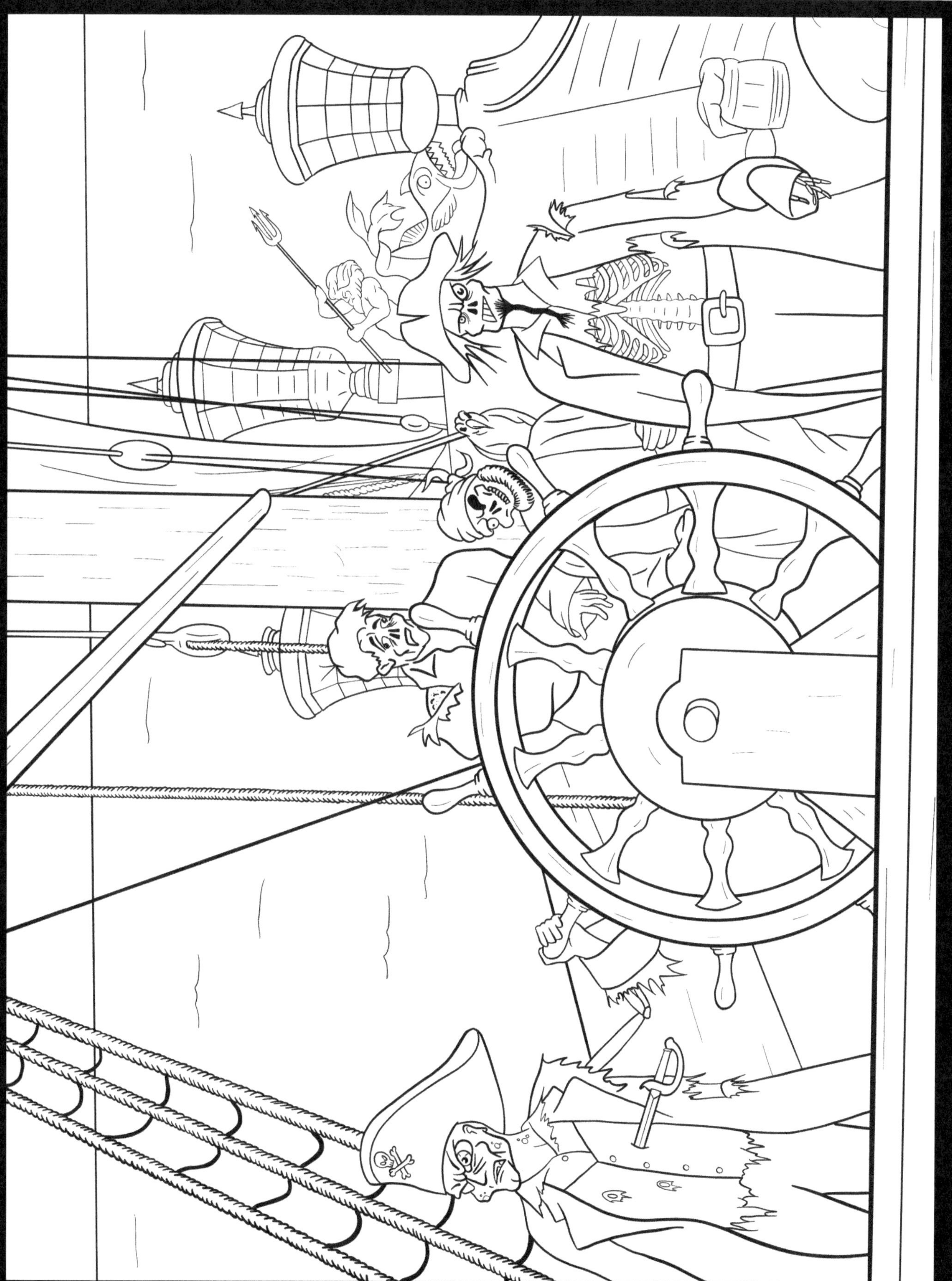

By The Power of Grey Matter!

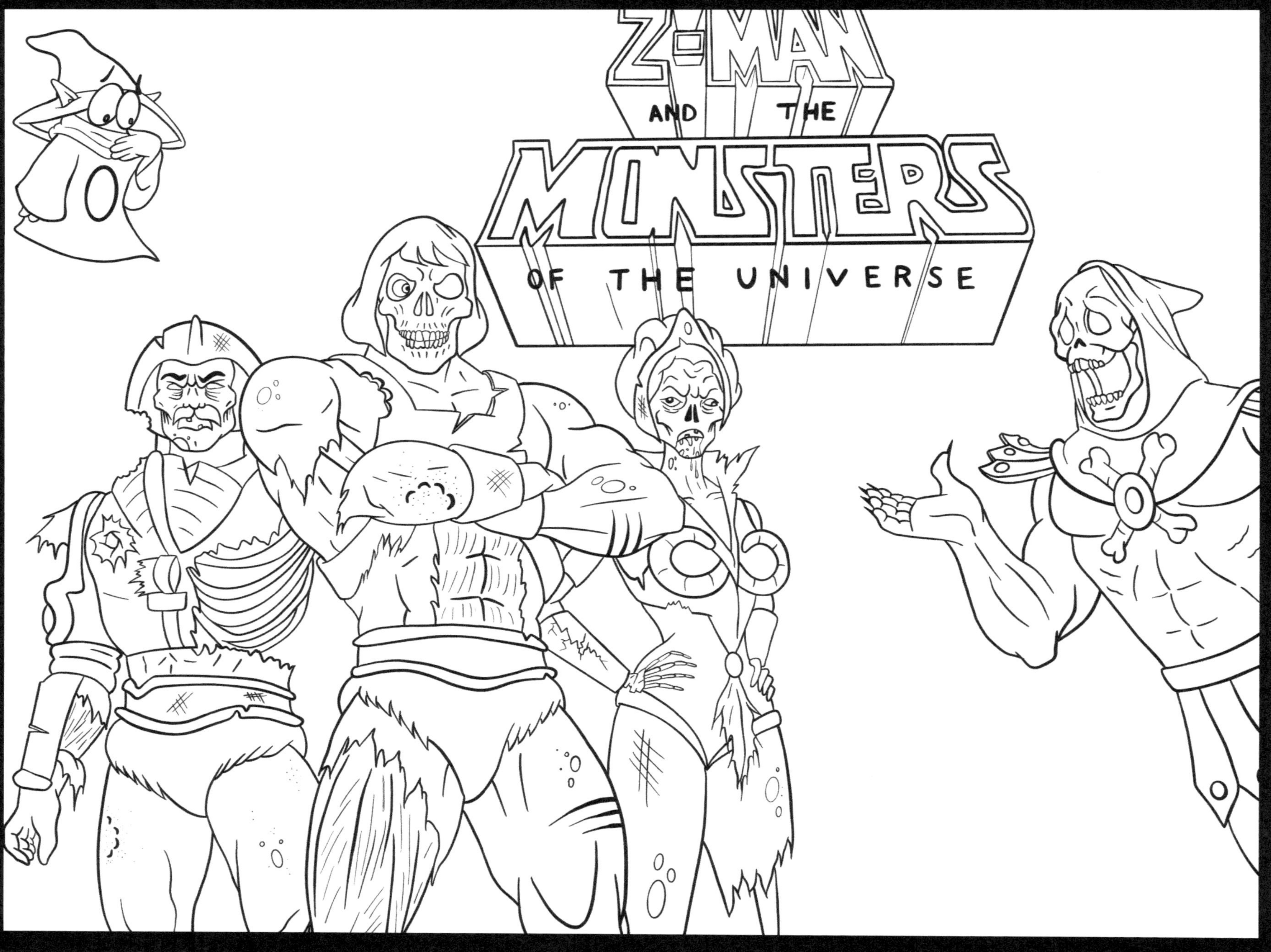
Z-MAN
AND THE
MONSTERS
OF THE UNIVERSE

Koo-koo-ka-choo, Mrs. Robinson

MIKE NICKILLS-LAVRENCE TOMBMAN
PRODUCTION

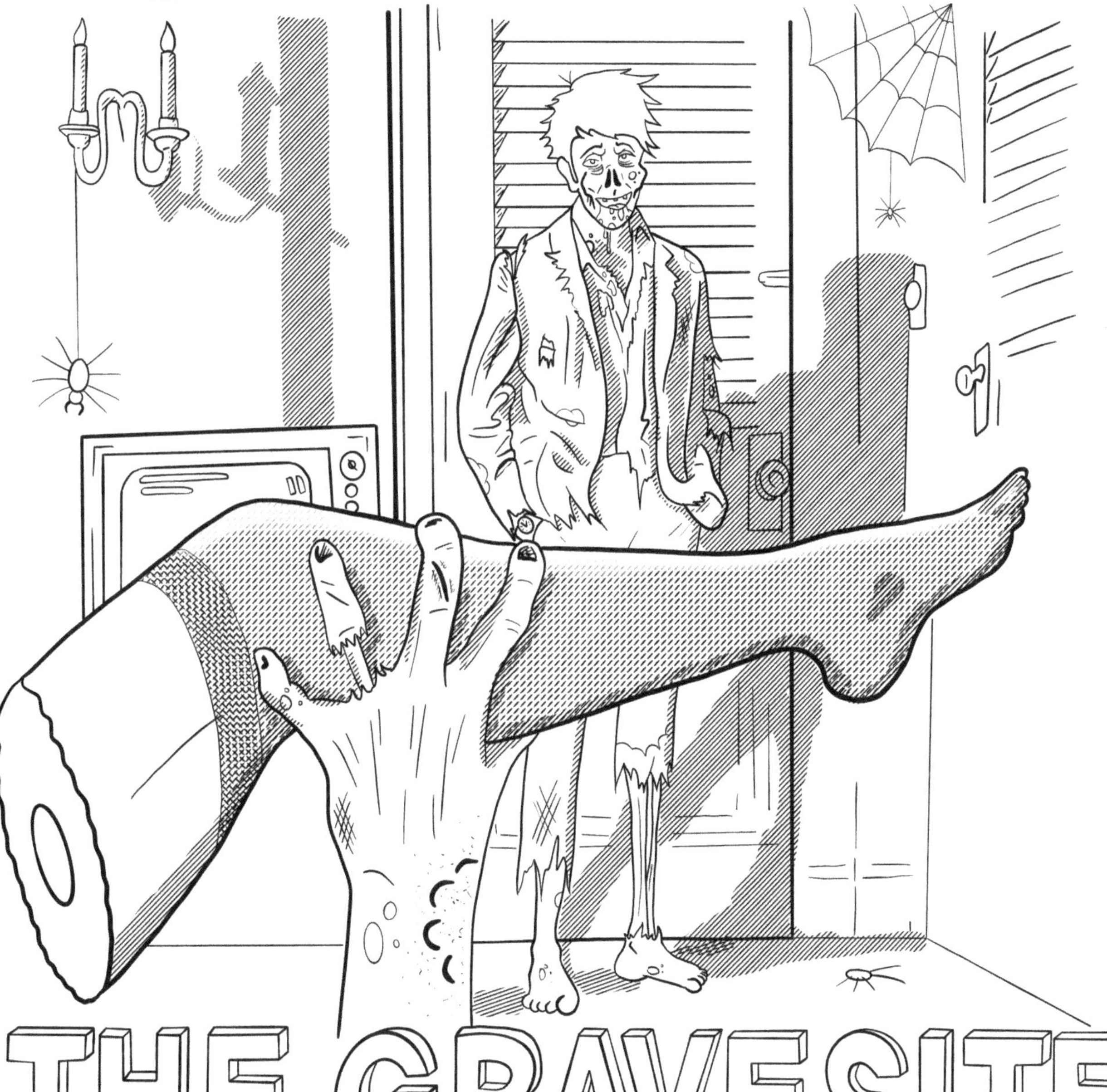

THE GRAVESITE

ANNE BANCRYPT - DUSTED HOFFMAN - KATERINE ROTS

I wonder if comedians taste funny.

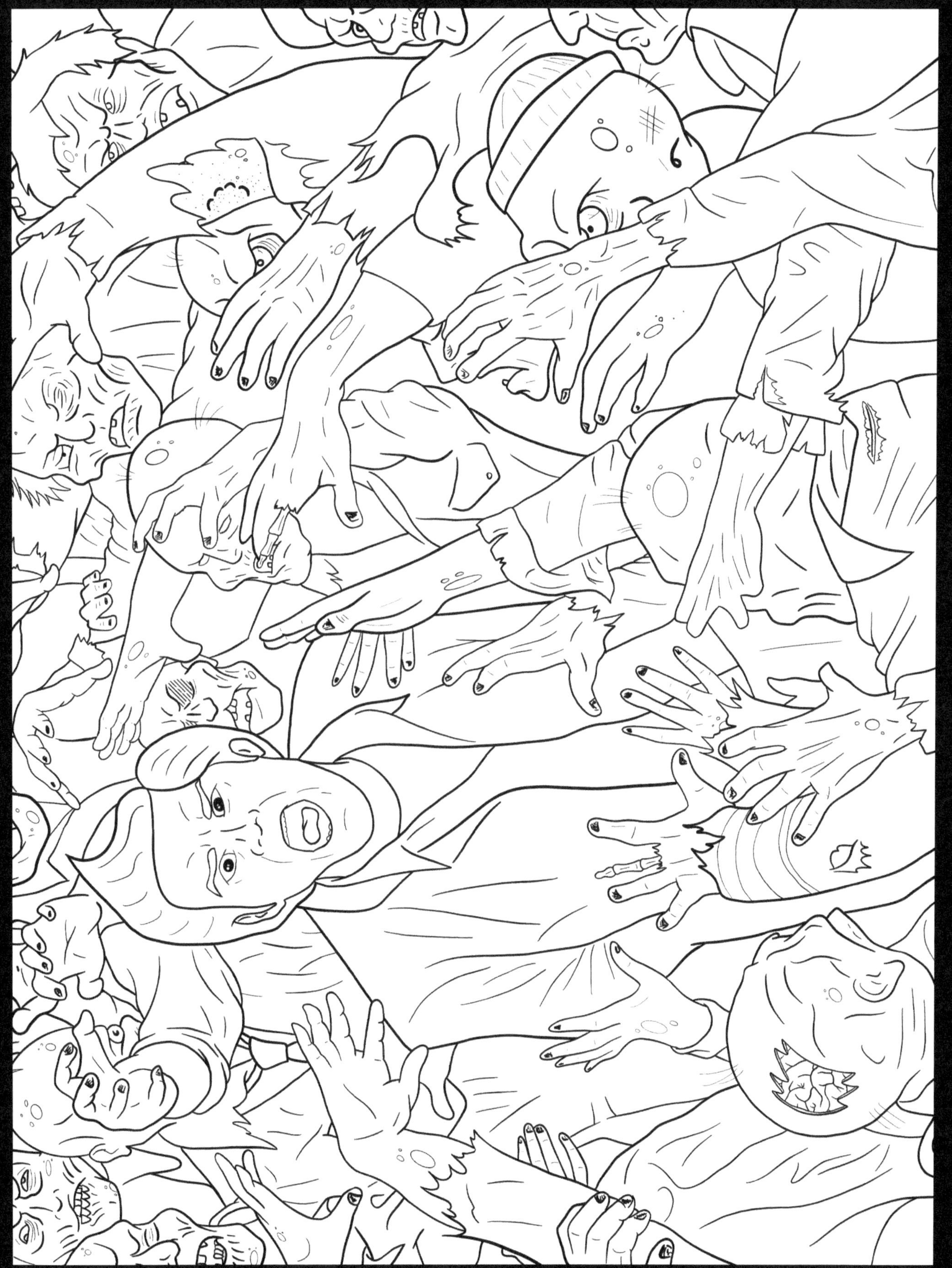

So no one told you unlife was gonna be this way.
CLAP - CLAP - CLAP - CLAP

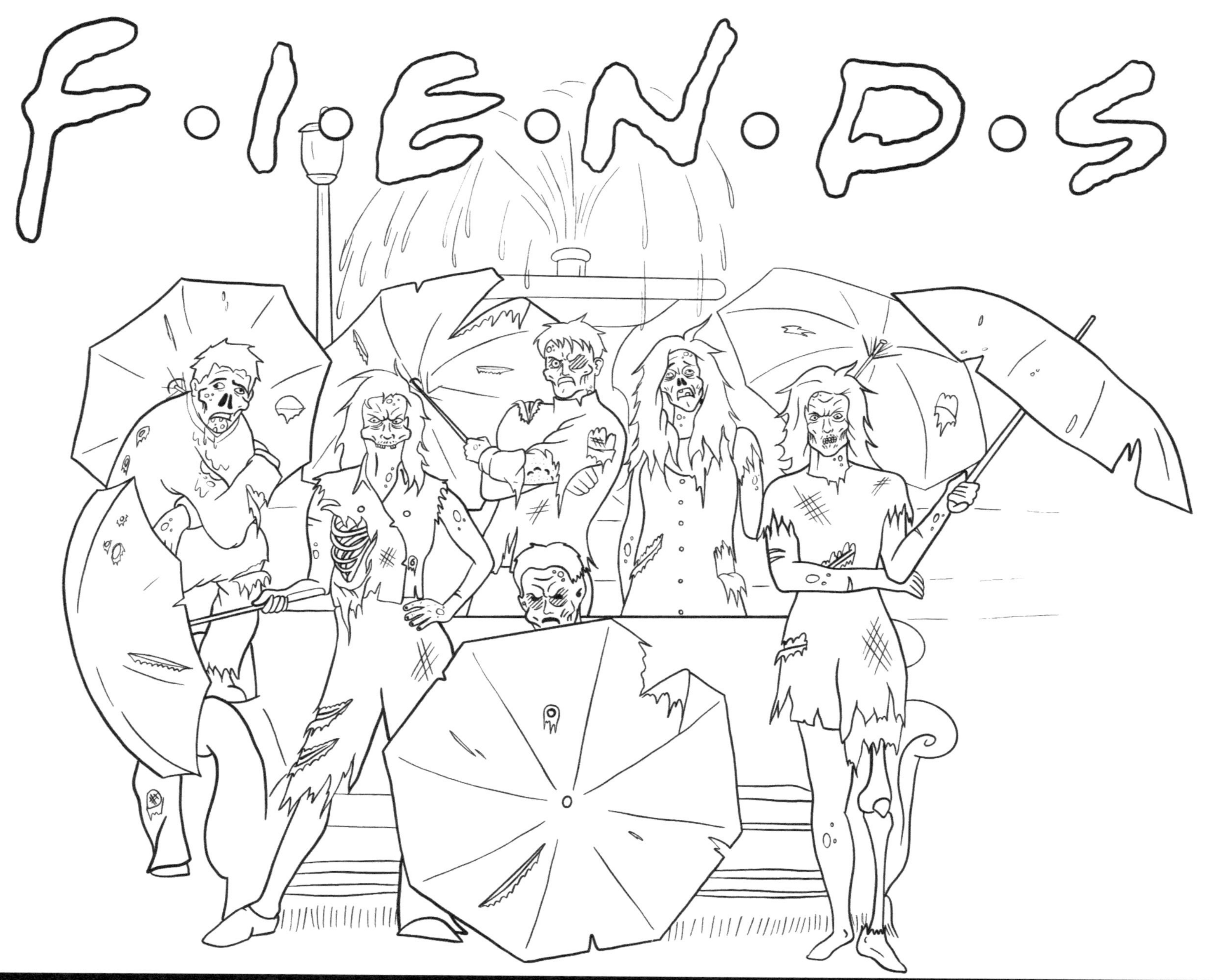
F·I·E·N·D·S

Strange things are afoot at the Circle K.

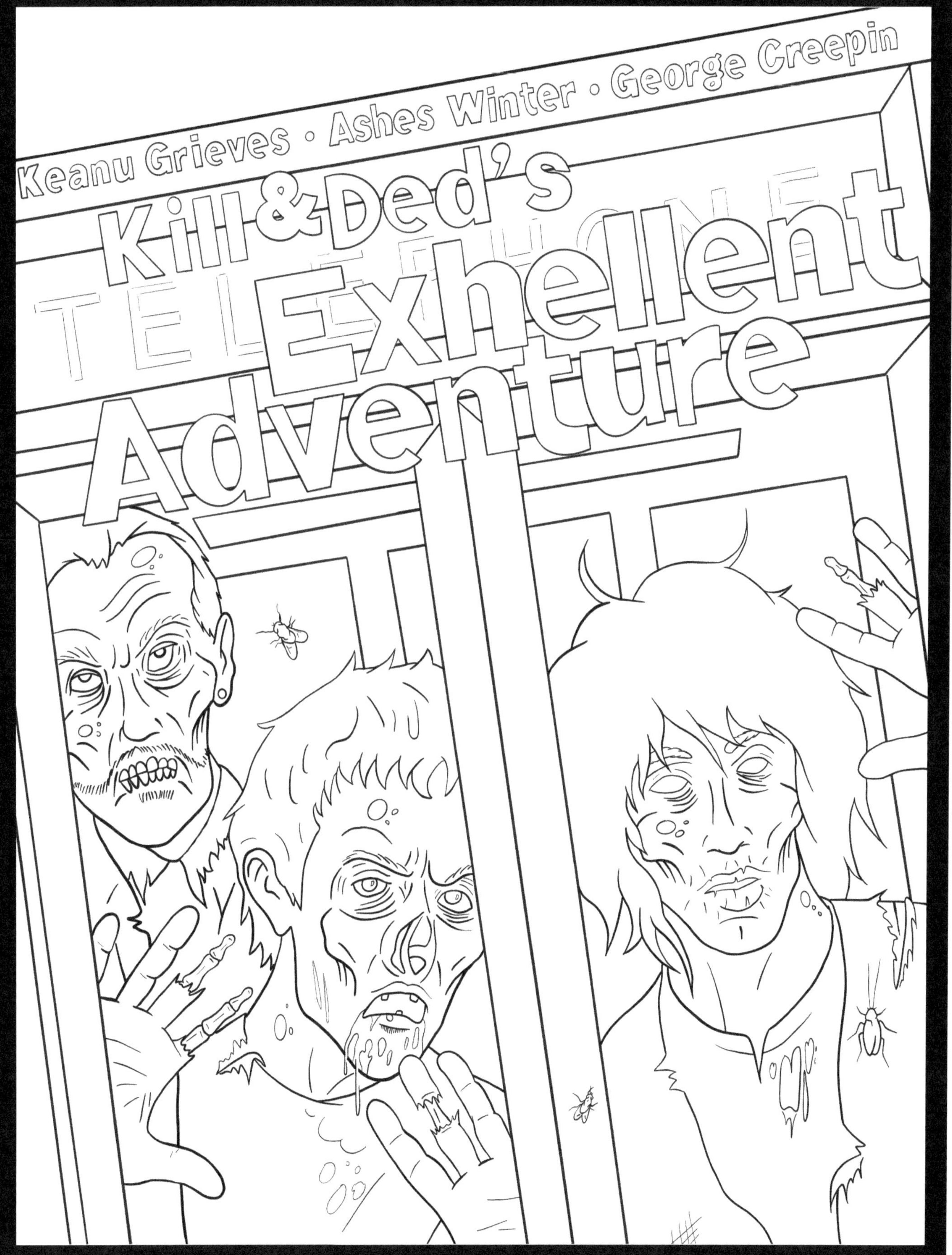
Keanu Grieves · Ashes Winter · George Creepin
Kill & Ded's
Exhellent
Adventure
TELEPHONE

Would she still pass the Bechdel test if she ate a man?

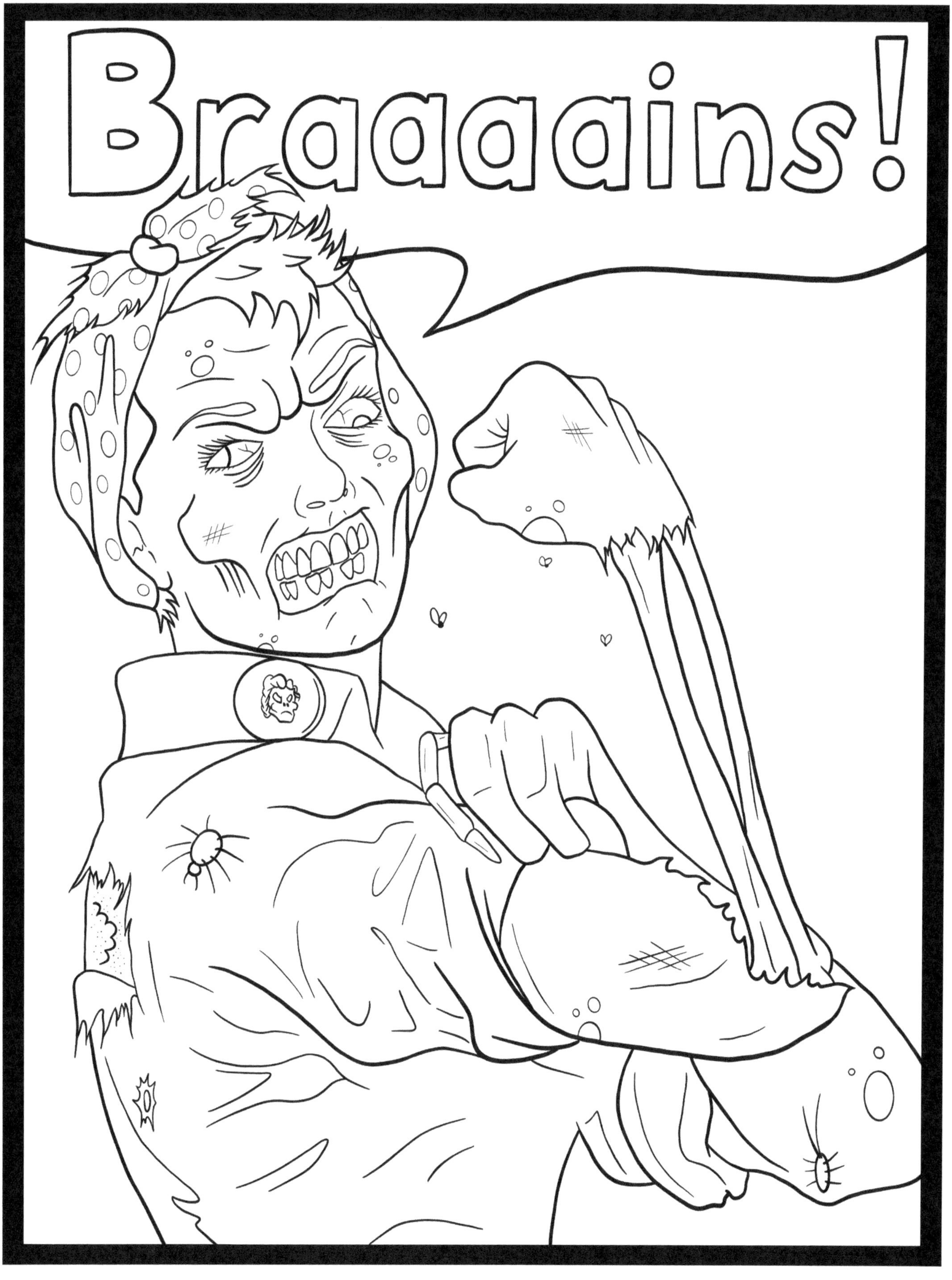

Braaains!

"The greatest trick the devil ever pulled was convincing the world he didn't exist."

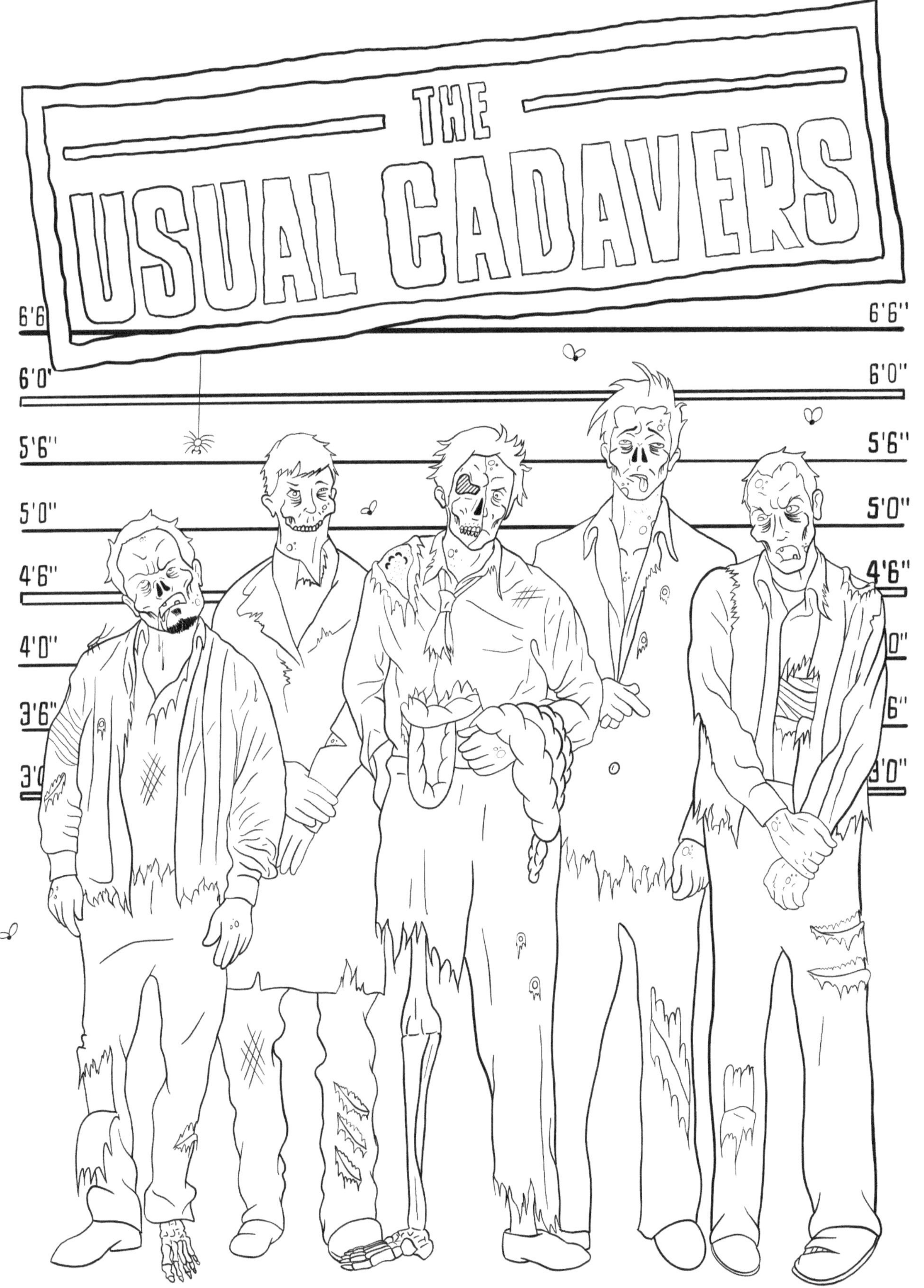
THE
USUAL CADAVERS
6'6"
6'0"
5'6"
5'0"
4'6"
4'0"
3'6"
3'0"

I was going to make a joke about
Napoleon Complexes...

...but it fell short.

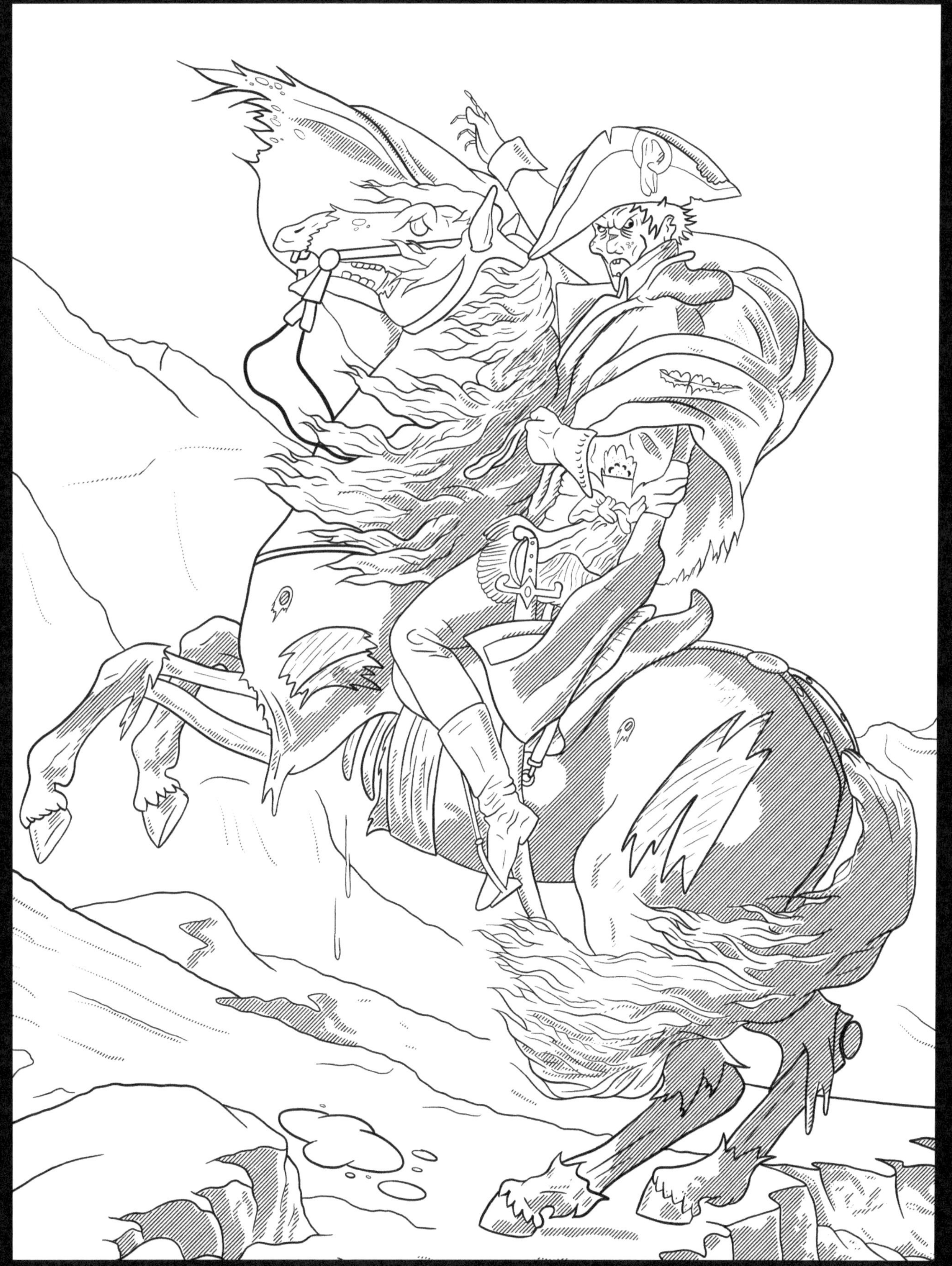

DOODLE: These zombies need faces.
Creepy faces or silly faces? You decide.
But you should definitely draw them some faces.

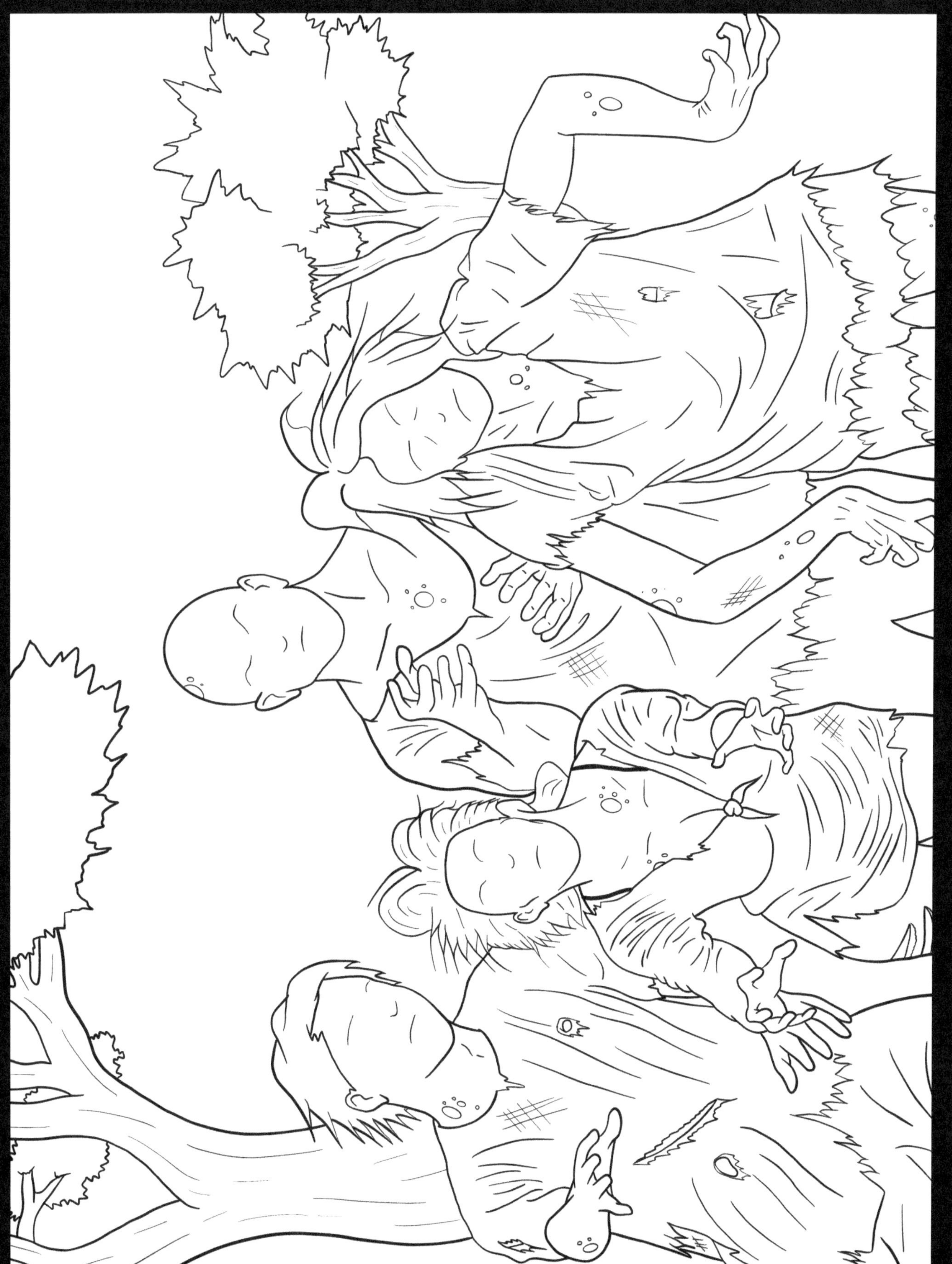

Next thing you know ol' Jed's a walking dcad
kinfolk said
"Oh God! RUUUUNNNN!!!!"

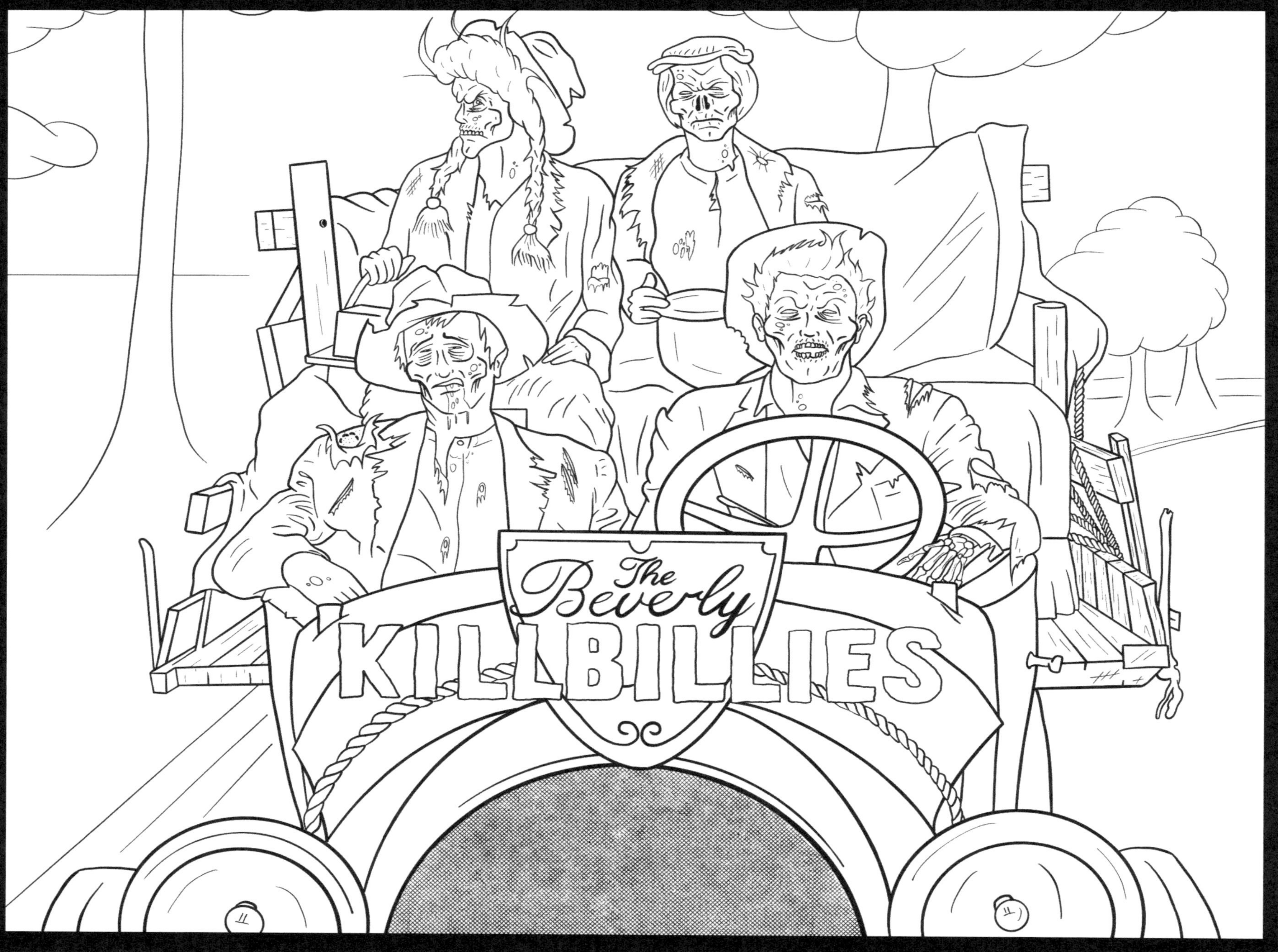
The Beverly
KILLBILLIES

How did we never notice that despite all that gunfire nobody ever died?

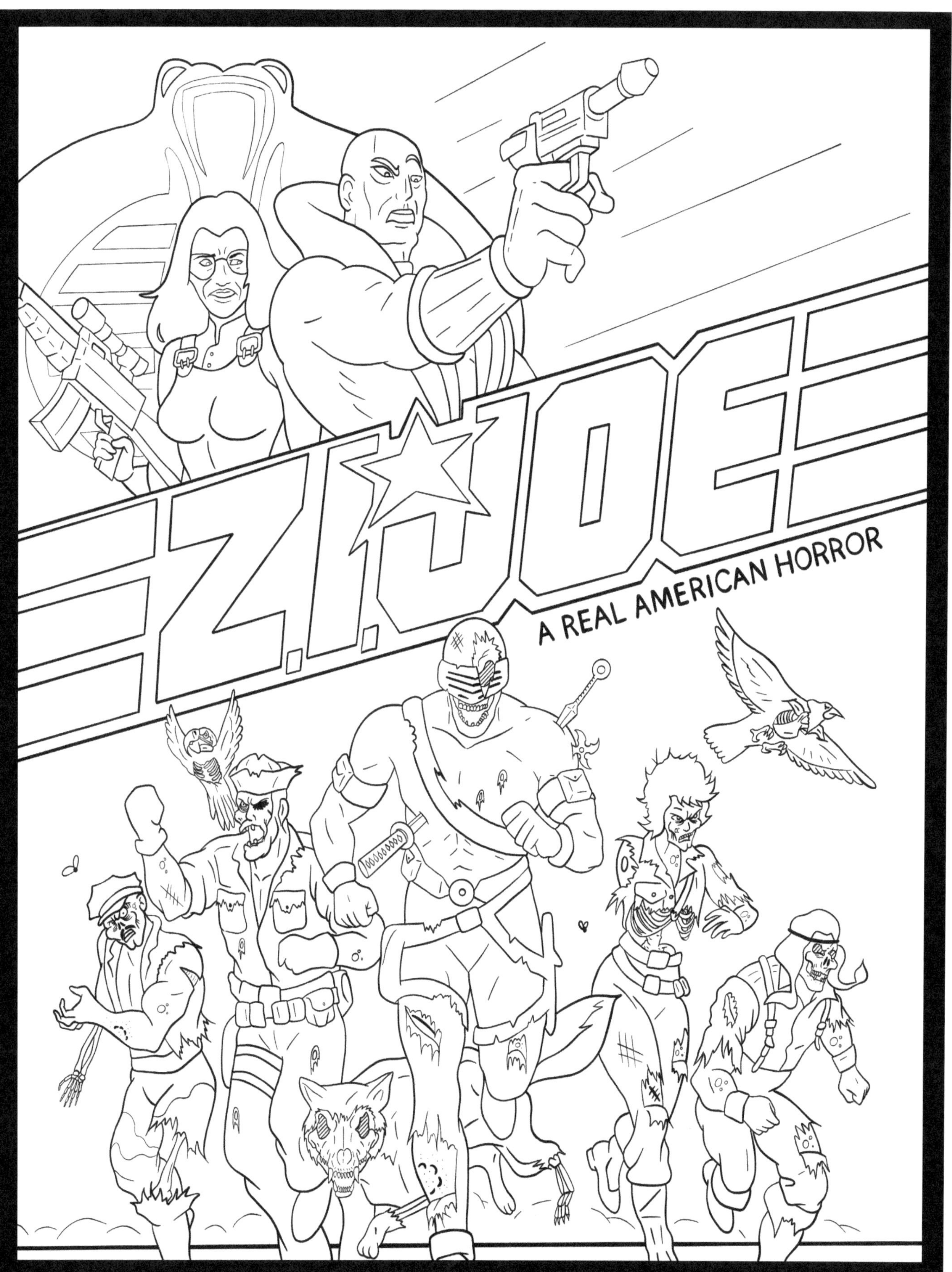
G.I. JOE
A REAL AMERICAN HORROR

Throw me a frickin' bone here.
No really. Throw. Me. A. Bone.
I'm hungry.

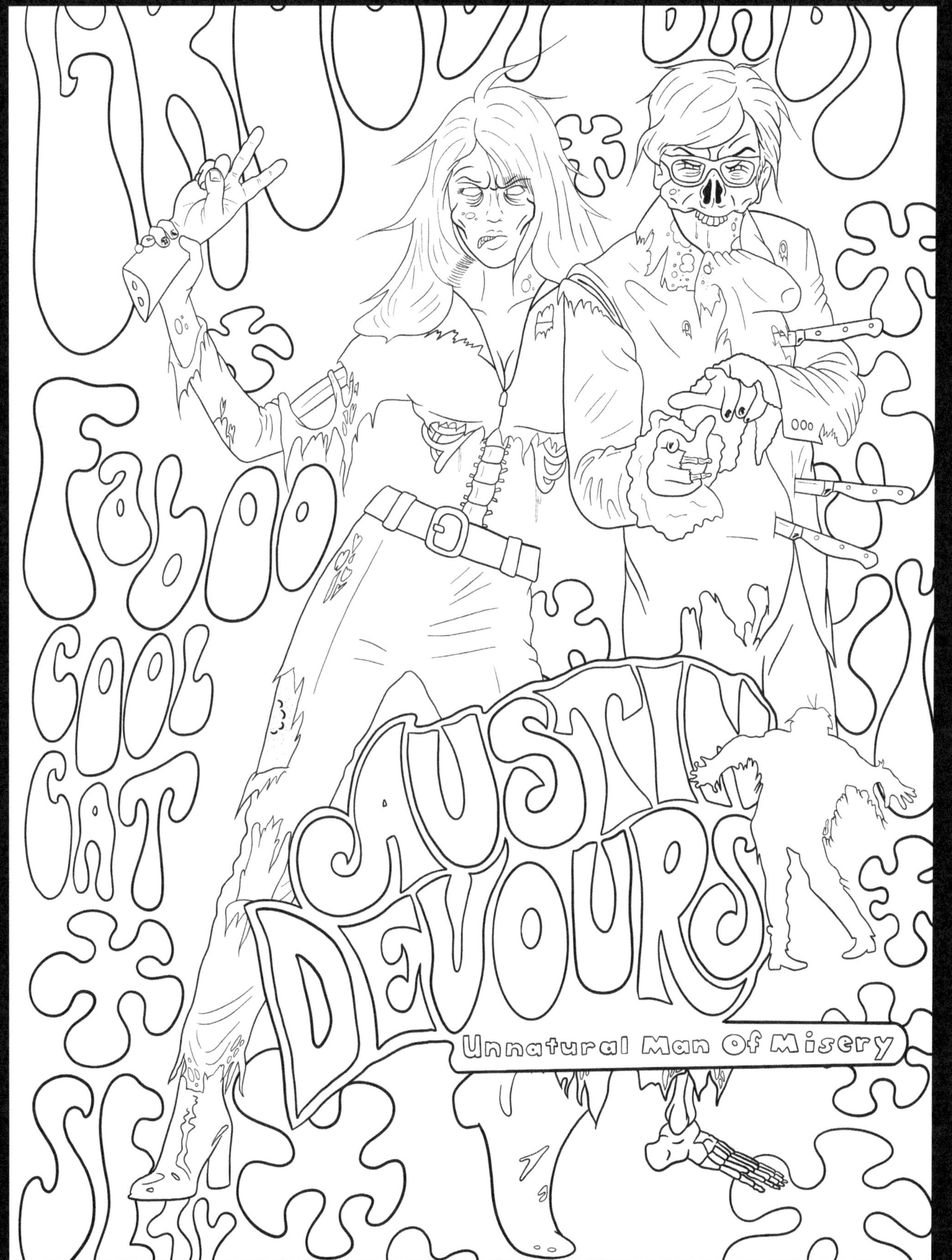
Faboo
Cool
Cat
Austin
Devours
Unnatural Man Of Misery

DOODLE: This zombie is about to take a big bite out of... what?
Draw his next meal.

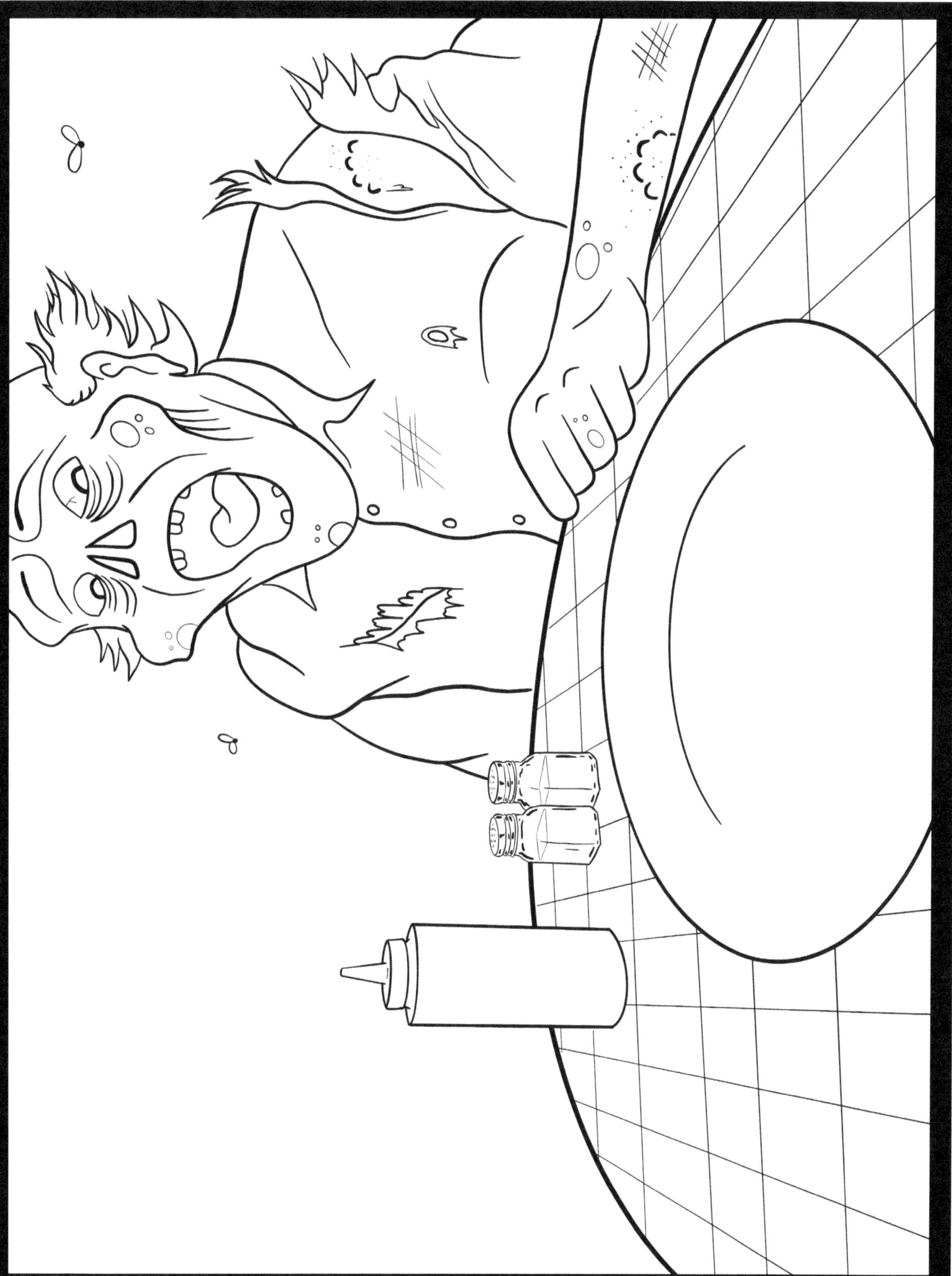

Bone spurs won't get you out of this one.

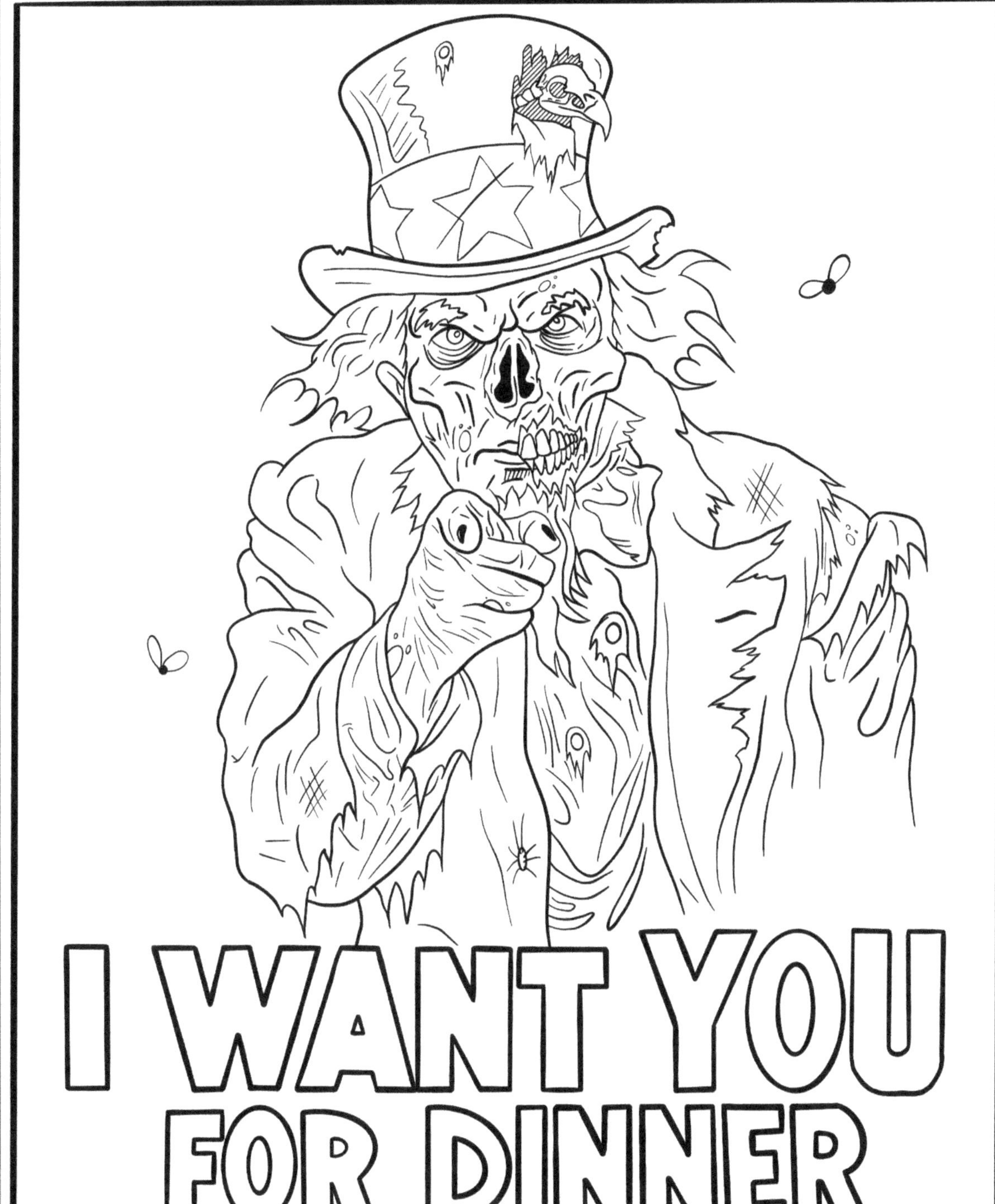
I WANT YOU
FOR DINNER
NEAREST REANIMATING STATION

Cap'n Be 'Merica and his famous hexagonal shield.
What? He looks like who?
Nope. Never heard of him.

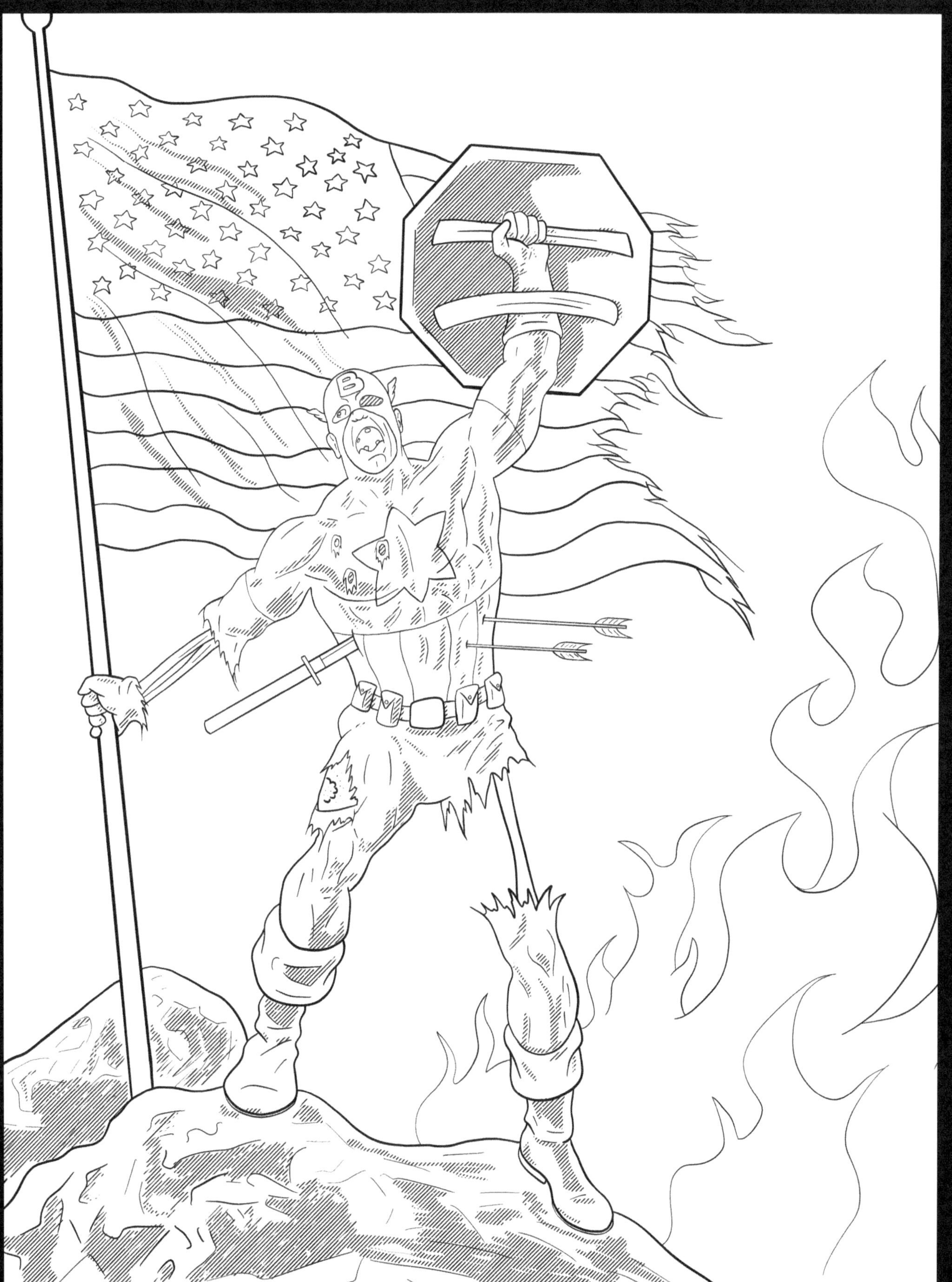

B

www.ingramcontent.com/pod-product-compliance
Lightning Source LLC
LaVergne TN
LVHW080249110826
845148LV00023BA/874

* 9 7 8 0 5 7 8 8 0 0 1 3 4 *